CUPID'S ARROW

LOVE INK

LEE SWIFT

CUPID'S ARROW

For Titus Love, matchmaking is much more than a hobby – it was the family business. Being the grandson of Cupid himself, Titus is obsessed with restoring his grandfather's good work and leaves Olympus to secretly work his magic in Dallas's hottest new tattoo studio, Love Ink.

Detective Derek Stone doesn't believe in love. Betrayed by a former lover, Derek views the sentimental emotion as a weakness that almost destroyed him vowing never to give anyone that power over him again.

While investigating a string of grisly murders, Derek discovers one common thread – all of the victims were clients of Love Ink and its owner, Titus Love. But when Derek questions his gorgeous suspect, their passion ignites and Derek discovers that the world is bigger and darker than he ever knew.

Something evil has come to Dallas, and only a hard-boiled detective and the new god of love stand in its way.

Copyright 2012 Kris Cook
Edited by Chloe Vale
Cover Art: Petra Leitner

eBook ISBN: 978-1-937249-06-9

❀ Created with Vellum

To Chloe Vale, a very dear friend and supporter, who always stands by me with encouragement, advice, and a nice dose of reality whenever I need it. You've done some really heavy lifting on this book, and I will be forever grateful. Thanks for the long hours and many phone calls.

PROLOGUE

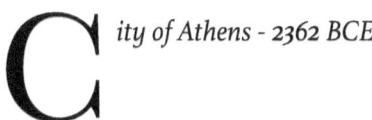 *ity of Athens - 2362 BCE*

Prometheus believed in fire.

Light and life came from fire. Fire, both visible and invisible, had been his gift, his legacy to man.

Fire would now be his death.

His limbs shook. Gods, he hated this. How long had it been since he felt weakness? Now he was drained, his soul shaking against his immortal bones, pain wracking through him.

They surrounded him, his most devoted followers, the very humans he'd gifted with fire and elongated life circled him, each with a hand on his naked chest. Stolen ambrosia flooded their bodies, bringing them close to the god he was.

Daphne. His sweet Daphne, with blonde ringlets and the breasts he'd loved to caress. She'd been his high priestess. Now her sweet face brought him death.

Would the other gods dare to leave Olympus to liberate him from this horror once they realized he'd been taken?

"Give over, teacher." She skillfully used everything he'd taught her about pulling life from the world around her to drain the fire out of him.

He fell to his knees, the strength leaving him, the light given him by his Titan parents flowing out of him and into the humans—*his humans*. He'd molded them from clay, forming their bodies and giving a vessel to their spirits. Man, his creation, his love.

"Master, this is for the best. We'll be gods now." Daphne kissed him with her traitorous lips. "Thank you, my love."

With only a single flicker of his spirit fire remaining, he slumped forward.

Man, his creation. Man, his enemy.

His eyes closed, the dark coming. "Take the rest," he choked out.

"No, my dear. Soon we'll feed you a little ambrosia. We need you alive."

He wouldn't die today or tomorrow, but death would come for him eventually. Until then, he would live in cold and blackness, his body providing fuel for their immortality.

As Daphne and the lesser priests enchanted his chains with the power they'd taken from him, Prometheus took his place in the dark and dreamed of vengeance.

1

D allas, Texas - Present

RETURNING from his fresh fuck with the cute bartender who worked at Secrets on Cedar Springs, Wiles Underwood put his key in the lock to the penthouse.

Samuel Barnes met him at the door, a sad smile on his face, which meant Wiles might have to blow his goddamn benefactor tonight to ensure the gravy train kept rolling his way.

"Where's my gift, baby?" he asked in his sweetest tone. Wiles often knew what people were going to say before they even said it. It was a skill he'd had his whole life. For years, he'd tried to figure out how to use it to his advantage. Like everything else in his life, it was just another useless trick.

He would've known what Sam was going to say next even without his special ability.

"No gift tonight, kiddo. We need to talk." Taking a seat on the sofa, Sam pointed to the leather chair opposite him.

Fuck.

For nearly a year, things had been perfect for him with this cash cow. He'd enjoyed a roof over his head, a large weekly stipend, a brand new BMW, and much more. The sex was lackluster, but he didn't give a damn. Tricks were a dime a dozen, but Sam's thick stacks of Benjamins made it easy to stay.

Time to turn on the charm.

"Sounds serious, lover." He sat next to Sam on the sofa instead of the chair, as the bastard had directed him. Taking the fucker's hand, he squeezed. "Tell me what's wrong."

"You're right. This *is* serious, Wiles." Sam pulled his hand free and scooted a few inches away. "I don't know how to say this, but I've fallen in love with someone."

He could see a spark in the prick's eye that hadn't been there before. Even with rage rolling through him, he knew he needed to present a calm front. "I'm happy for you." He reached for Sam's hand again, and this time the asshole didn't resist. "Really, I am honestly happy for you."

Sam smiled. "I'm so glad. What we've had has been great."

"Have you told your new boy about me?" he asked cautiously.

"I have."

"What does he look like?" He squeezed his sugar daddy's hand, hoping to find an off-ramp from this shitty detour. "Sharing might be fun."

Sam shook his head, untangling his hand from his. "There won't be any sharing. Not anymore."

Every muscle inside him tightened. "Are you kicking me out?"

"It's time to end this. We both know that."

His pulse felt like a jackhammer in his veins. *I can't be homeless. Not again.* "No. I don't know that."

The douche frowned. "You don't love me, and I don't love you."

Careful, Wiles. "That's not true. I do love you," he lied. "I love you very much."

"You may think you love me, but you don't. Love is so much more than fondness or chemistry. I know that for a fact. I'm happy now, happier than I've ever been in my entire life. I want the same for you, but you can't stay here."

Anger and panic clawed at his insides. "How long before I have to go?"

"I've already called a realtor to find you an apartment. He'll be here in the morning." Sam leaned forward and patted him on the back, making him feel like a dog. "Of course I'll pay the lease for the first year for you."

The millionaire scum's offer amounted to crumbs. "I'm okay, though a little sad. You mean the world to me, but I want you to be happy. Whoever this guy is, he must be something special for you to feel this way about him."

"He is very special."

"That's great, Sam." Uncertainty ripped his mind into a thousand shreds. "Give me some time to get my head around this. It's going to be tough at first. You're an amazing lover. I'll just have to learn to be satisfied as your personal assistant."

"No, Wiles. You can't be my assistant. It wouldn't work out. Besides, you were more of a companion to me than anything else. Until you find a job, I'll pay your bills. I owe you that. I still would like us to remain friends."

Instead of pounding the prick's head into the floor, as he wanted, he kept his cool. "Thank you."

Sam's shoulders sagged, making him appear even more repugnant than before. "I'm sorry about this."

He hugged the bastard, though it sickened him. "I really am glad you found true love."

"Someday you will find it, too." The creep kissed him on the cheek, which turned his stomach.

He sent the idiot a fake, toothy smile. "When did this change of heart start, baby?" He needed to get to the bottom of things to turn this catastrophe around. "You've been acting different for about two weeks."

"I guess I have." Sam leaned back and smiled. "What a whirlwind. I met Jonathan right after I got my last tat."

"It's the one on your chest, right?"

"Yes." The rat pointed to where the ink was under his shirt.

"Let me see it again, sweetheart. Take off your polo."

"I don't think that's a good idea." Sam stood. "I'll sleep in the guest room tonight."

"I'm not trying to seduce you, boss," he said, shoveling another load of crap at the asshole.

"Bullshit," Sam laughed. "I know how naughty you can be."

"Fine." He pasted his best smile across his face and looked up at his evaporating meal ticket. "Can't blame a guy for trying. I thought a good-bye fuck was in order, but since your heart belongs to another, I guess a good-bye drink will have to suffice."

"Thank you."

He left the couch and stood next to the traitor. "At least promise that you'll go with me to look for an apartment."

"Okay. I surrender. We'll go in the morning."

"You're the best," he said as sweetly as he could muster. "Let me get us some drinks so we can toast to your new life and my new home."

"You got a deal. What poison would you like?" Sam asked.

"Sit down, baby. I'm the better bartender of the two of us."

The snake nodded, returning to his seat on the sofa.

"I'll be right back." His mind raced through his choices, and one kept moving to the top of the list.

He brought Sam his favorite drink loaded with several pulverized pain pills. He'd thought about crushing some of his stash of crank and adding it to the mix, but didn't. Once finished here, he would need to fire up his pipe to clear his head. The cocktail he'd made for himself was nothing more than vodka on the rocks.

"A toast, my love," he said, making sure to keep his tone light. "To you and your new life, Mr. Barnes."

"And to you, Wiles," the Judas fucker said, holding up the glass in his hand. "I wish you all the best."

They clinked their Waterford tumblers together, and the lovesick bastard downed the special brew in just three swallows.

Wiles took a single sip, barely holding back the maddening frenzy inside him.

"How about I fix another for you and you can tell me more about this new man in your life?"

"Sure thing." Two more glasses put Sam into a full stupor in under an hour.

Pleased with his handiwork, Wiles guided the cheat to the bedroom and onto the mattress.

"You shouldn't have fucked things up." He stripped Sam of his clothes.

"P-Plea...you can't...we can't...do this...I love Jonathan..." The fool's words slurred.

He kissed the tattoo with the three circles and arrow in the middle, marking the start of this entire disaster. Strangely, it gave his lips a little bite of static. *Don't get distracted, Wiles. Stay on plan.* "Shhh, baby. I'll take care of you."

Sam smiled idiotically up at him. "A-Apartment sh-shopping will be fun, kid. You'll see."

"I'm not going anywhere, lover, but you are," he whispered in the dying asshole's ear.

"I am?" Sam slurred. "Where...to...kiddo?"

"To the grave, fucker. To the grave."

The goner's eyelids widened.

He kissed the jerk on the lips. The slackness his tongue found there thrilled him.

"That's right, asshole. You're dying. I gave you enough pills to down an elephant. If lover boy shows up to look for you, I'll be sure to fix him a drink too."

Sam became slightly agitated, but his eyes closed and his breathing became shallow. The drugs were working perfectly, as expected.

Fascinated, he stared at Sam as the man's life slipped away, fading little by little with each passing second.

After the deed was done, Wiles noticed the ink on his dead patron's chest start to move. Transfixed by the vibrating design, he placed his hand on top of it. A rush of heat and electricity shot up his arm and into his chest. Had Sam's sudden change of heart come from this tattoo? There was no way this was just skin art. But what was it? Light? Magic? Current? Whatever it was, the shit felt extremely potent, and he wanted another hit.

He put his mouth to the ink on Sam's skin, licking the lines. His action created something between him and the tattoo, a kind of invisible conduit allowing him to siphon the hot power from the corpse into his own body. As more and more of the invisible stuff pumped into him, his senses expanded and came alive. He could really see for the first time.

"What the fuck." He looked down at the light swirling around him. Regretfully, he didn't have the luxury or the time to ponder what had just happened to him. His terror-stricken brain shoved the supernatural shit aside for the more pressing matter—saving his ass.

He was completely justified for killing Sam, but he was also totally fucked.

After a few minutes, an intense calm spread through him. There was work to do. "This looks a lot like a suicide." Yes. That would save him. What would seal the deal was a suicide note.

Grabbing a pen to try to write the message, he realized the flaw in his new plan. He couldn't forge Sam's unique handwriting, with its curls and circles. God knew he had tried to do it before with some blank checks he found in the asshole's nightstand.

He slapped Sam's still face. "Motherfucker. You did this—you and your goddamn tattoo artist. Why didn't I hold a gun to your head and make you write a suicide note? I need it to be in your fucking chicken scratch and not mine."

The time had come to cut his losses and make tracks.

He was about to toss pen and paper aside when his hands began to warm. Light shot from his fingertips and words suddenly began appearing in black ink on the page—in his benefactor's scribble. He looked at the pen, still in his hand and not on the paper.

His wish had come true.

Detective Derek Stone looked down at the lifeless body of the fifty-six-year-old male, Samuel Alvin Barnes.

Visiting the county morgue and the horrors it presented didn't disturb him. In his line of work, you either learned how to turn off your emotions or you ended up at a desk shuffling papers for the homicide unit. Besides, he'd learned from Bill—his one and only ex —that feelings were completely overrated and often dangerous.

In an odd way, death actually made sense to him. Unlike his fucking curse, he could get his head around the morbid concept. A human body was nothing more than a mix of fluids and tissues animated for a time by a beating pump called the heart and an electrical battery called the brain. Either due to old age, illness, accident, or homicide, in the end, everyone—rich and poor, powerful and weak, good and bad—ended up a corpse.

Dr. Elizabeth Littlefield turned on the big light above the stainless steel table holding the cadaver. "Exactly as I told you on the phone, this is a suicide." The curvy blonde medical examiner donned surgical gloves. "Nothing more."

It might look like a suicide on the surface, Liz, but I can think of a million other possibilities it could be.

He scanned the man's body, mentally noting the tats on his arms, chest, and ankle, as well as the old scar on his chin. "Did you find any bruising on the murder victim's skin or other drugs in his blood?"

"Murder victim?" Her eyebrows shot up. "You think this is a homicide? He left a suicide note."

Hoping to avoid a lengthy, pointless argument with her, he didn't answer.

She was clearly undaunted by his silence. "Derek, don't do this. You're just off of probation. You don't want to screw up again, do you?"

He would never call Liz a friend. In fact, he had no friends. That suited him just fine. Still, she and her husband, Steve, had been at his house several times following the Bill years. During the breakup, she and her hubby had knocked on his door, but he'd refused to let them inside. Steve quit coming with the doc after a couple of times. Even Liz stopped dropping by after a few months of receiving not a single invitation to come inside. He'd thought she'd taken the hint that he wanted only to deal with her on a professional level, not a personal one, but he'd been wrong. Next month would be three years since the split, and Dr. Littlefield still called at least two times a week, though he never called her back. Heaven help him, he genuinely admired the woman's never-give-up-on-a-lost-cause attitude, but opening up to her—or anyone else for that matter—wasn't going to happen. Ever again.

"I'm here about Barnes, Doc. You going to answer my questions or shall I go find someone else who can?"

She shrugged and looked back at the body. "Besides his blood alcohol being off the charts and the high levels of opiates in his system, nothing." She touched Barnes's sides with her gloved hands. "No external wounds, bruising, or lacerations. This man downed an entire bottle of pain pills, drank two or three of martinis, and went to bed. That's all, Derek. Samuel Barnes was dead in less than an hour. Look at me."

He turned his gaze away from the deceased to the blue-eyed woman.

"I'll say it again, Detective. This is a clear-cut case of suicide."

"Maybe."

She sighed and took off the latex gloves.

He flipped out his pad and reread what he'd jotted down about this case already. The deceased man had been found four hours ago in his penthouse on one of the city's premier streets, Turtle Creek. Barnes's fortune, which had come from his deceased parents, pushed past the hundred million mark. That kind of dough had granted him full access to the superrich around the world and had put him at the tip-top of the A-list in the gay community in Dallas. The usual suspects were many—jilted lovers, old business partners, former employees, and more. Barnes likely had many enemies that would've wanted him in the ground.

His cell vibrated. He looked at the number on the screen and felt his jaw tighten. *My babysitter. Great.*

"Stone here," he answered.

"Where the fuck are you?" His new partner's voice came through the receiver loud and clear.

"Morgue. You?" He flipped the page on his notepad and studied his scribblings. Barnes had one living relative, a nephew who lived in Paris on the trust fund from his mother, the vic's dead sister.

"Shit. You're wasting your time at the ice house, Stone." Michael Vende's angry tone didn't impact him in any way. "You're going to get me busted if you don't fucking chill."

"What do you want, Vende?" he asked flatly.

"I want your sorry ass back at the unit and pronto. The boss wants this case closed ASAP."

The boss, Homicide Unit Commander Lieutenant Gray, might have it in for him, but he wasn't about to rush the investigation.

"I'm not signing off until I'm certain this was a suicide and not a murder. Sloppy police work is something I won't do."

Vende lashed out. "Don't tell me you're getting one of your fucking ESP episodes again, Stone. That's what got you busted in the first place."

"Actually, I was put on probation for slugging another officer." He'd broken the guy's nose. Those around thought his action had been way out of line. But his fellow officers had only heard the rookie ribbing him about the Sammons Case. They hadn't seen the young cop's thoughts like he had, images of him actually pissing on the whole lot of them as they knelt in front of the creep. Telling his peers that would have landed him on a shrink's couch. It was bad enough the rumors about his curse still floated around the unit.

Right now, Derek's sixth sense was firing on all cylinders just being next to Barnes's ice-cold body.

"Listen carefully, Miss Cleo," Vende said. "Barnes was found in his bed by his personal assistant with an empty bottle of gin and an empty bottle of pain pills. End of story."

"I have some questions for the assistant."

"Not necessary, Stone. I took a full statement already from Mr. Underwood. He found Barnes this morning when he arrived for work. He says Barnes had been battling depression for years. Apparently, last night it got the best of him. And before you ask, his assistant has an ironclad alibi."

"And the nephew?"

"His alibi is even more unquestionable. He was home in Paris at the time of death. That's Paris, France, not Paris, Texas. Got me?"

He mentally clicked through the facts he'd already collected on the victim. Given what he'd witnessed himself the other night, this didn't add up to a suicide—note or not. No way. "I want to talk to Barnes's nephew."

"You've got to be kidding. The guy won't be here until late tonight to make arrangements for his uncle's funeral. The only thing left to wrap up is for Liz to file her report, which she told me she should have done within the hour. This case better be in the drawer and closed by tonight."

Arguing with Vende wouldn't be productive, so he remained silent. His partner wouldn't be open to his conclusion that this was a murder, no matter the evidence. Not yet anyway.

He thought about telling his babysitter what he'd seen at a nightclub recently, but decided against it. A hunch wasn't evidence Vende would be receptive to.

He'd seen Barnes at one of the premier gay dance clubs on Cedar Springs Road during one of his infrequent trips out to land a one-night stand. That had been just a week ago. The millionaire had been dancing with a beautiful man. The two seemed completely enamored with each other. The grin he'd seen on the victim's face that night didn't support the assistant's claim that Barnes had been depressed.

"Are you still there, Stone?" Vende asked.

"I am."

"Do what you have to do but do it fast. You have all you need there?"

"Almost," he stated.

"Fine. Once you get back to your desk, we can wrap this up and file it away." Vende's tone didn't soften. "What do you say, Stone?"

He actually couldn't blame the guy for his frustration. His partner was a good man, a great detective, and had a long, successful career ahead of him. The lieutenant might have chosen Vende to shadow him because they were two of the few openly gay detectives on the force, but he doubted it. Gray's unspoken rule was no fraternization inside his team, gay or straight. That wasn't an issue for him with Vende. Even though his partner was quite handsome, with caramel-colored eyes, dark hair, and a muscled frame, Vende wasn't his type. The chemistry wasn't there. Besides, his partner was too idealistic and gung ho. And it didn't take telepathy to see Vende was a man who wanted commitment. That would never be Derek. Ever again.

"I'll talk to you later, Vende." He clicked off his cell, ending the call.

Liz shook her head. "Derek, you've got to let this one go."

"Why? If this is a murder, this guy deserves justice, doesn't he, Doc?"

"It is not a murder," she snapped.

"What if you're wrong?"

The doc exhaled and shook her head. "My report will classify his death as an overdose."

"Give me forty-eight hours before you file it."

"I will be uploading my findings into the system in an hour."

"I'll split the difference with you." Calling her by her first name wasn't something he did regularly, but desperate times and all. He needed her help on this one. "Wait until noon tomorrow...Liz."

"Don't try to play me, Derek. I know you quite well." She knew him better than most. "Fine. After that, you're on your own, detective." She turned on her heels and exited through the metal swinging doors.

He looked at the digital clock on the wall. Eight minutes after twelve. The doc had just bought him a day to keep the file open.

He scanned the body on the table. For a man in his fifties, the vic's ripped abs indicated numerous weekly visits to the gym. Jotting down that fact in his notepad, he looked at Barnes's face. The goatee was likely an attempt to detract from the lack of hair on his head.

What am I overlooking?

Once Liz filed her report, the nephew would pick up the body for burial, then the crime techs' pictures and the ones taken at the morgue by Liz's team would be all he had left to examine. There had to be something everyone was missing. What? Maybe nothing. Maybe what his mother called his gift, and he called his curse, had finally misfired. That would be a welcome relief. Then he could be normal, like everyone else who didn't hear people's thoughts from time to time or sense things that no one else ever did.

He sighed, praying his fucking vibes would be hushed once and for all. Closing his notebook, he took one last glance at Barnes. The sight of the ink on the dead man's left pec made his unwanted gifts go into overdrive.

Fuck!

The tat was of a triple spiral with an arrow resting in the middle of it. Not unusual for the average onlooker, but his second sight wasn't average. As the ink began to vibrate and change colors on the bloodless skin, he knew the vic hadn't committed suicide.

Barnes had been murdered.

2

Titus Love lifted his foot off the pedal to the tattoo machine, and its humming noise stopped. In his very long life, he'd never felt more alive than he did running Love Ink, the trendiest tattoo studio in Dallas.

The finished art on his latest customer, Paul Crane, filled him with pride. The *extra* he'd put into it caused the ink to shimmer in the ethereal plane.

"All done," he said.

The young man sat up from the table and positioned his leg to get a better view of the new tat on his ankle—a triple spiral with an arrow in the middle of it.

He grinned broadly. "It's perfect."

"I'm glad you like it."

The mortal man could only see motionless body art. He, on the other hand, watched the lines vibrate and change color. *Yes, it is perfect!*

"You're so talented." His customer tilted his head back. "My boyfriend's gonna flip."

Boyfriend? He knew better. When the guy had entered the studio, there'd been no hint of passion, not even slight affection, on his aura. With the current tat on the man's ankle, all that would change.

He smiled, motioning his cousin, Kyros, to bring the aftercare paperwork. "Paul, I'm going to give you some instructions about what you need to do to take care of your tattoo. You don't want to get an infection."

"Sure. I'll do whatever you say." The guy's eyes glazed over, clearly feeling the magic of the symbol on his ankle.

The first tats he'd made from the ink enchanted by his granddad's arrow had taken several hours before fully activating. This customer's tat had sped to life in seconds, continuing to grow. His divine skills seemed to have improved greatly since opening the shop. He hoped his grandfather, Eros, the god of love, would be proud of his magical abilities.

Paul's tone turned soft and thoughtful. "Mr. Love, do you know the guy that works at the coffee house on Maple? He's amazing. I go there every Tuesday and Thursday for a double-shot espresso. His name is Jeff."

"Is he your boyfriend?" Titus asked, watching the magic swirl around his customer's entire body.

The man's smile evaporated in denial, but his voice trembled, exposing the truth. "No-o-oh."

"Maybe he should be."

Paul cocked his head to one side and nodded absentmindedly.

He reveled in his job. How could his granddad have walked away from it? Thinking of family caused his guilt to rise, twisting his stomach into knots.

He glanced back at the locked desk drawer containing the arrow he'd swiped from the family's trophy case. It was important to stay off the radar of everyone back home. So far, he'd only enchanted seven of his customer's tats, counting Paul's. He'd wanted to help many more customers with their relationships, but couldn't. Being selective was the only way to keep his new venture going. He could only place the triple spiral and arrow with the divine ink on the ones most in need of true love.

Shaking off his bad conscience, he got back down to business. "Paul, your contact information is correct?"

The man nodded, clearly in a daze from the spell.

"Good. Your tattoo will turn to disaster if you don't follow my instructions. I'm going to apply ointment and then put a bandage on it. Leave it on for at least three hours. That will keep bacteria away. When you do remove it, you need to wash your tattoo. Use lukewarm water and liquid antibacterial soap..." As he continued giving instructions, he watched the man's aura go from the dark gray-blue that he'd entered the studio with into a bright red.

Kyros handed him the paper. "Here it is, boss."

All of Love Ink's customers swooned over his cousin. No wonder. Six foot five. Wavy blond hair. Kyros looked to be in his late twenties but in truth was only three years younger than him at two hundred and twenty-six. Greek demigod—or he would have been if the whole clan of ancients hadn't closed up shop long ago out of fear.

He had more in common with his cousin than any of his other family members. Besides, Uncle Notos, Kyros's dad, was one of the key supporters, albeit under the table, of the dream to renew the family business. When Uncle Notos had asked him to take Kyros with him to Dallas, it was easy to say yes, and besides, he loved his cousin's company.

"After a few days, Paul, you'll notice some peeling and possibly a little scabbing."

"It's gonna scab?" The mortal sounded worried.

He handed him the written instructions. "Maybe, but there is no need to panic if it does. Apply a warm, moist compress to any scabs that appear for about five minutes two times a day to soften them and they'll eventually come off."

"Two times a day. Got it." The guy dropped his foot back to the table and rested his head on the pillow.

Before placing the bandage over the new tattoo, he gazed into it and silently instructed: *Draw this mortal to his true love—and his true love to him.*

The three spirals began to spin on the man's skin and the arrow turned a bright red. *Excellent.*

"Even if you start itching, don't scratch. And definitely don't pick."

Then the tat shimmered and split in two: one part flying off the man's ankle and out the shop obviously to the coffee house, the other sending out energy waves over the mortal's entire body, guiding him to the guy who would change his life forever.

"You sound more like a doctor than a tattoo artist," the young man said.

"And how would you know?" Kyros donned a new set of gloves. His cousin would finish cleaning the station and disposing of the rest of the hazardous waste. "You said this was your first tattoo."

The human smiled. "It is. And I love it!"

"Kyros, please don't tease the customers." He walked over to the red biohazard container and disposed of his gloves and ink caps. He returned to the table where Paul remained. "Take good care of it. And enjoy. Any issues, just give me a call."

Paul jumped to the floor. "I'm so glad I found your webcast, Mr. Love."

"Call me, Titus."

"Sure thing." His customer walked to the door of the studio, but turned before exiting. "I'm going to tell everyone I know that they need to come to you for a tattoo."

"Please do."

After the human was gone, Kyros turned to him. "Cousin, one question."

"Shoot."

"How do you pick the ones for your *special* tattoos?"

"It's their auras that tell me. The ones with the dark colors need love in their life in the worst way."

"And the mortals with black?" Kyros could see auras and knew what they meant as well as he could.

Black. The hopeless. The saddest of all humanity.

"We've not had one of them come into the shop," he answered.

His cousin shot him a knowing glance. "But if one ever does?"

Even though his grandfather's arrow had incredible power, to cut to the heart of someone with such hardness would be next to impossible. Even back in his best days, Eros would've never attempted it.

He'd just gotten started in the family business, and it would be foolish to try to pierce through such pain and suffering. "We'll cross that bridge if a person like that shows up in the studio."

Kyros shook his head as he cleaned the station. "A total waste of ink if you ask me."

"Maybe." Still, he'd come to bring passion back to the world, and even the hardest heart deserved a chance at love. "I've got a ton of paperwork to finish back in my office. Do you mind covering the front?"

"No problem. I'll call you if we get busy."

Two hours later, he emerged from his office. "Any customers?"

"It's been dead," Kyros stated. "You just missed several of your fans. Five of them. Said they would be back tomorrow to meet you in person."

His webcast had been the best marketing tool of the shop, garnering them several customers. "I'm headed to the fridge for a bottle of water. Want one?"

"Please."

When he came back with their drinks, he found his cousin talking to one of the sexiest men he'd ever seen in his very long life. Then the divine spark hit him right in the heart, showing him the man was a descendant of one of the ancient oracles.

Six foot four, dark hair cut razor short, grapefruit-sized biceps, square jaw. If he didn't know better, he would have thought the mortal was a god. A stud, through and through, just like he liked them. Was he gay? This was the gayborhood. Or perhaps he was only lost.

Then his gut tightened. The man had the darkest aura he'd ever encountered since opening the shop, nearly as black as the waters of the river Styx.

What could have broken the light of such a man?

"There you are. This is your next customer." Kyros motioned him over. He heard his cousin's voice in his mind. Telepathic communication was a power his entire family possessed. "Apparently the bridge has arrived, boss. This guy's aura is as dark as I've seen." Aloud, he said, "Derek Stone, this is our esteemed owner and the most talented tattoo artist in the state, Titus Love."

The man turned to him. His eyes, the color of rich chocolate, didn't blink. Was he studying him?

"Nice to meet you, Mr. Love." His voice, deep and rich, could command Titans to their knees and satyrs to the bedroom.

When the mortal extended his hand, he met it with his own. The man's touch sent sparks up and down his spine. "Please call me Titus."

"Titus, then." Derek's hand left his, and he flipped out a badge. "Call me Detective Stone."

"What the fuck is this?" Kyros snapped.

Titus held up his hand to quiet his cousin. "What can I do for you, detective?"

3

___

Derek couldn't quite put his finger on why just being near his one and only suspect had his fucking sixth sense itching. Nothing clear yet. Still, he had a strong feeling that Titus Love had secrets, and those secrets were the key to solving Barnes's murder.

After seeing the tattoo on Barnes's chest, Derek was certain that it was the key to solving this case. A quick look at the victim's bank statement led him to Love Ink.

Both tattoo artists were stunning. Even though Titus's employee was certainly male-model gold, Derek couldn't stop staring at the owner of the place. One thing for certain, Love overflowed with sex appeal. The man's multicolored eyes mesmerized him, the most prominent shade being a deep violet. He also spotted flecks of gold and silver on Titus's irises. The kissable brute's thick lips tantalized him. Even the man's bronzed muscles were perfection. The black tank Love wore exposed his arms. On his left one was an impressive dragon tat. On his right, symbols circled his bicep that looked tribal. The guy's cargo shorts were loose, keeping Derek wondering what was hidden underneath the cotton. The leather sandals on the man's feet seemed more suited for the beach than a place of business. Still, this tattoo parlor was not your typical mom-and-pop shop, and Love wasn't your typical entrepreneur.

"I've got a few questions for you, Mr. Love."

"It's Titus."

"Nice place you've got here, Titus." He glanced around the space, noting first the exits. *Better to play it safe than to play it dead.* The front door he'd entered through was one. The door in the back of the space with the exit sign above it was two. There was a hallway to his left that likely led to another way out.

The furniture wasn't from a big-box store's hodgepodge collection. The ultramodern decor with chrome, glass, simple lines, and black leather must have cost a small fortune. The walls weren't covered in drawings of the artist's best tats, which he'd expected. Instead, a feast for the eyes decorated the surfaces.

On the wall at the far back were clearly the works of Touko Laaksonen. The explicit gay themes of muscled men enjoying each other were beautiful. To his right, an Andy Warhol, but not one he'd ever seen in any book or magazine. Still, with its bright colors and simple lines, it was clearly a work of Warhol or a damn good imitator. To his left in an alcove, a marble statue of two naked men embracing contrasted the pop and modern art in the room.

"You like my statue, Detective?" the sexy guy asked.

"Looks like a priceless piece of art. Where did you steal it from?"

Love smiled. "My mother's living room. She's a bit of a collector of such things." Titus's easy demeanor would trap nearly any gay man and just as many women. His suspect's calm manner was rare. Most people became nervous whenever he arrived, especially once the badge came out—guilty or not.

Best to get on with what I really came here for and stop looking at this man's amazing eyes. "Do you remember a Mr. Barnes? Mr. Samuel Alvin Barnes? You put your tattoo gun on him."

"It's not called a gun, Detective. Yes, I remember him."

"When was the last time you saw him?" He scanned the male beauty for any sign of nervousness. None appeared.

"Kyros, can you check the computer, please?"

The other man nodded and went to the table with the laptop on top of it.

Love looked back at him, causing his insides to boil with lust and heat. "Would you mind, Detective, if we continue our discussion back in my office? It would be much more comfortable."

Discussion? Love is one cool operator.

"Lead the way." He followed the seductive beast, enjoying the view of the man's ass.

Titus opened the door, stepping aside and motioning him in. "After you."

Having his gun holstered under his jacket, he mentally went through what to do should his gorgeous suspect try to get the jump on him. Caution had always been Derek's middle name, and his pistol had saved him more than once in some very tough spots. He stepped inside, placing his fingertips on his Beretta's grip.

Thankfully, he didn't have cause to bring the weapon out. Love walked past him and sat down in one of the black Barcelona chairs in front of the desk meant for guests instead of the larger chair meant for the occupant of this office. It seemed as if the man was trying to put him at ease. Didn't Love realize that he was in hot water, not the other way around?

"What's happened to Mr. Barnes, Detective?"

A man's office gave intimate clues into what kind of person he was. Love's sacred place didn't disappoint. Like the main room they'd just left, this space was warmer, more inviting. Could this be brilliant staging by a psychotic mind? "What makes you think anything has happened to him?"

"You wouldn't be here unless he was in some kind of trouble...or worse."

"It's worse, Mr. Love. Barnes is dead." Again, he studied the man for any body language that might incriminate him. Nothing. His face clouded not with guilt but with what appeared to be genuine sorrow.

"How, Detective?"

"Apparent suicide," he said, not about to share his suspicion that Barnes had been murdered.

Love closed his eyes. "Fuck."

"Did you know him well?"

"Not really." The man shook his head and opened his eyes. "That doesn't make sense."

"Why do you say that?"

Before Love could answer, Kyros entered. "You gave Mr. Barnes his tat two weeks ago."

"What's your name, buddy?" Derek asked.

"You already know," the guy snapped. Clearly he wasn't about to win Kyros's vote in a popularity contest.

"Full name," he said, pulling out his notepad. "For the record."

"Swift. Kyros Swift."

He jotted down the name, planning on running it through the system. "Were you here when Mr. Barnes got his tattoo from Titus, Kyros?"

"Call me Mr. Swift." The guy's sarcasm wasn't lost on Derek. Kyros was no coward that was for certain. "No. I wasn't here."

"Where were you at the time?"

"Visiting my mother."

"Her home? You have her address?" His sixth sense was firing on all cylinders. What were these two men hiding?

"She doesn't live in the states." Kyros's eyebrows shot up. "Anything else?"

"Yes." Finding out if Swift had left the country wouldn't be difficult. "Where does your mother live? What country?"

"Are we suspects, Detective?" his primary suspect asked.

"Direct. I like that, Mr. Love."

"Please, call me Titus."

"Okay. Titus. I'm still sorting out evidence about Barnes's demise. It's too soon to make any conclusions."

A chime sounded from the other room.

"Customer," Kyros stated. "My parents live in Litochoro, Greece. If you want more from me, Detective, just let me know. If I need to contact my lawyer, let me know that, too."

"Will do, Mr. Swift." He couldn't help but admire the man's toughness. There wasn't an ounce of cowardice in Kyros.

The guy exited the office to greet Love Ink's next client.

He turned to Titus, who was gazing at him with those fucking gorgeous, unsettling eyes.

"So is Kyros right? Do we need an attorney, Detective?"

He didn't like Titus's expression. Gone was the ease he'd seen in him earlier. Now, his face darkened with a threatening storm bubbling to the surface clearly from deep within.

"This isn't a joke. A man is dead. My job is to get to the bottom of things."

Titus didn't blink or move for a very long, dark pause. The silence was broken by his deep, hushed tone. "Go on. Ask your questions, Detective."

Arguably, Love might've killed Barnes. Motive, means, and opportunity had to be determined. "Can you tell me your whereabouts over the past few days?"

Normally, solving cases was all that mattered to him. Once on a scent to truth, he would never give up until found. Sleep became less and less. The tick of the clock taunted him until justice was served. He loved his job. Always had. But now something new punched through his mental armor, something hidden.

"I was here most of the time. At home only to sleep, Detective."

"Was anyone with you?"

"No. As you know, Kyros was at his mother's until yesterday."

"What about at your home?"

"I live alone," his suspect answered.

His hunger for this man was more intense than he'd ever felt before. But if it turned out that Titus was trying to deceive him, even a one-time fuck with the sexy beast would be off the table. He'd played the fool once with a liar. Never again. A silent prayer turned the inside of his head into a punching bag.

Please let him be innocent.

4

Wiles traced his finger over his latest victim's body.

Pride swelled inside him. Another task well done. In a strange way, he was sad that no one would ever know the murders, which now numbered three, were his doing. In fact, none of the fatalities would ever be deemed homicides. Fooling the cops about Sam Barnes's death had been a piece of cake, especially given his new talents.

"Thanks buddy, but I'm done with you." He kicked the naked corpse of Jeff off the bed. The guy had worked at a coffee shop on Maple, and though not Wiles's real target, the hunk had been a nice side treat. He turned to the other unbreathing man, stroking his lifeless arm. "But I still need something more from you, Paul."

Of course the stiff didn't respond.

Stiff? The irony made him smirk.

Few ever got his sense of humor. It took a sophisticated and highly intelligent mind like his to understand. He longed for peers, but doubted he would find anyone of his caliber, at least not in Dallas.

With Sam now out of the picture, Los Angeles was his next stop. Hell, with the supernatural voltage he was about to drain from Paul

Crane, who knew what heights he might reach. "Movie Star" had a nice ring to it.

The tiniest bit of the strange energy he'd gotten from Sam remained inside him. Thinking about his former sugar daddy made his blood boil. *What a motherfucker.*

But his road of hard knocks had finally paid him a hefty dividend. All he had to do to switch on the power was concentrate fully on what he wanted, and hocus-pocus, it happened.

He'd used a big portion of the invisible energy he'd gotten from Sam getting into Detective Vende's head. He'd convinced the detective to accept that Sam's death was nothing more than a suicide. As the magic got used up bit by bit, his cravings for more intensified.

After Detective Vende's questioning, he'd activated more of the invisible energy to find another fix, another source. The hocus-pocus had led him to just outside of Love Ink, where he'd spotted Paul exiting the place.

His instinct was to follow Paul to the coffee shop. He'd watched his prey chat up the guy behind the counter like a lovesick schoolgirl. With his newfound magic, charming the two hotties into a three-way and snorting coke had been child's play. The sex had definitely been a blast, but the coffee shop stiff didn't have anything else he wanted.

Dead Paul here, on the other hand, did. Wiles smiled when he saw that tat on his victim's ankle. He deserved this advantage more than anyone. Until now, his life had totally sucked.

The ink of the three circles and arrow on the dead man's ankle vibrated and hummed.

He placed his lips on the tat. "Mine. All mine." Then just as he'd done with Sam, he licked the lines, drawing the hot power into his body.

Once the entire ball of power was inside him, he sat up and smiled. Willing only a sliver of the magic into the room, he used the glowing spark to erase all evidence of his presence in Paul's residence. The cops wouldn't be able to find a thread, a print, or DNA that pointed to him.

Picking up the plastic bag that held the rest of the coke he'd brought with him, he tossed it next to Paul's body.

Grinning, he gazed at the two men he'd just fucked and sent to the angels. "Sleep tight, my darlings."

DEREK WAS glad to see the unit empty, which was unusual for this time of day. Four o'clock. The extra time Liz had given him was ticking away, and he was no closer to proving Barnes had been murdered than he was when the day started.

He walked over to his partner's desk. Pristine. Nothing was out of place. Michael was more than a little OCD.

"Stone." The voice of the commander came from behind. The lieutenant was not pleased, that was certain.

He turned around and saw Lieutenant Mason Gray's eyes narrow into an unspoken challenge.

"Sir, do you need me for something?" he asked in a fashion that let his boss know he wasn't ready to back down to him or anyone else, for that matter.

"Glad you decided to finally show up today. My office. Now." The man—a born leader through and through—walked into his office, clearly expecting him to follow.

Derek couldn't get a clear read on Gray, which was odd for him. Despite everything, he still found the commander intriguing. The guy couldn't be much more than thirty-five, which was young to be in the position of head honcho of homicide in the Dallas Police Department. The three homicide squad supervisors were at least a decade or two Gray's senior. The lieutenant wasn't fazed by the age differences at all, coming into the group only five months earlier like an angry bull with flaring nostrils. The man had taken charge and demanded results from the get-go, which had gotten him a lot of DPD accolades. Even the deputy chief of the Crimes Against Persons Division had come by a few times smiling ear to ear since Gray's promotion.

Deputy Chief Moore had never smiled during his impromptu visits to the unit before.

Bracing himself for the barrage, Derek walked into the commander's office.

The lieutenant didn't look up from the papers he was reading. "Take a seat, Stone."

His mother's gift was dishing out a big dose of nausea in his gut. *Fuck! What now?* Deciding it best to wait and see, he took a seat.

Gray glanced at him for a flash, but then the commander went back to reading the file in front of him. Finally, the boss closed the folder and looked at him. "I just got off the phone with Dr. Littlefield about ten minutes before you arrived."

Liz. Crap. Had he lost the twenty-four hours they'd agreed to?

"And?" he asked flatly.

"You're a piece of work, Stone. You know that? It's bad enough that I have to put up with your bullshit, but now you're making sure to piss me off royally. Dr. Littlefield said she won't be able to file her findings tonight. In fact, she told me I could expect her full report by tomorrow afternoon at the earliest. Did you have something to do with that?"

Liz still had his back. "What's on your mind, Commander?"

"Don't fuck with me, Stone. I have your number. You've got one of your hunches on this Barnes case, don't you?"

Taking the lieutenant's bait wasn't something he was about to do. Not yet, anyway. So, he shrugged and folded his arms over his chest.

Gray frowned and shook his head. "You're a talented homicide detective. Why you want to fuck up a perfectly great career isn't something I will ever understand. It's all in here." The man patted the thick folder in front of him.

"Those are my records?" Derek asked.

"Unit records only, Stone. HR has everything else." The lieutenant looked past him. "There's the other half of this debacle now. Let's get him in here and see what we can do about this mess you've created. Officer Vende, get in here."

His partner entered and took the seat next to his. "Yes, Sir."

"I was just telling Stone that Dr. Littlefield won't be turning in her report until tomorrow. Do you know about that?"

"Damn it." Vende turned and faced him. "Derek, what did you do at the morgue?"

"My job," he stated flatly.

"More than that I would bet," their commander said. "Barnes had lots of friends at city hall, and they want this put to bed. So do I. Where are we on the case?"

Vende didn't look away from Derek but answered Gray. "Suicide. Open and shut. He even left a note. His assistant identified the handwriting as Barnes's, which our experts also verified after reviewing samples of his script in other documents."

"Stone?" the commander asked.

He met Gray's harsh stare directly. "I'd like to speak to his assistant."

"I'm not asking you what you'd like to do, Officer. I only want to know what evidence you've found to keep this case open. Am I making myself clear?"

"Crystal." Normally he appreciated Gray's directness. Not now. He needed more time.

"What do you have for me, Stone?"

"Barnes got a new tat not long ago. I spoke with the owner. He's hiding something."

The commander hit the top of his desk with his fists. "Why the hell would a skin artist want to murder Samuel Alvin Barnes? Were they lovers?"

"I don't know." His every instinct told him there was something there. He wasn't going to stop until he figured out what.

"Business partners then?"

"Unknown."

"You're treading on very thin ice, Stone. Very thin indeed." Gray turned to Vende. "You better make sure your partner gets this closed or both your asses will be mine. Understand?"

"Yes, sir." Michael stood.

"Good. Get out of my office, both of you."

Derek got up on his feet as his partner exited.

"Stone."

He stopped and waited.

Gray shook his head and then looked him directly in the eyes. "Bring me real evidence by tomorrow. That's it. That's all the time you have."

He nodded, feeling his internal clock begin to tick off the seconds.

"Now, get the fuck out of my face."

Without another word, he headed to his desk.

STARING at nothing in particular and lost to a million thoughts, Titus remained seated in his office. The detective had left an hour ago, but he was not forgotten.

Derek Stone's presence threatened to destroy his hopes, his dream. The man had vowed to return at a later time with more questions. The mortal's warning should've had him packing his bags and heading back to his granddad on his knees, confessing all and begging for forgiveness. But it hadn't. Instead, he actually was looking forward to his next meeting with the sexy guy even though the detective's aura was dark and his heart seemed closed.

"What's the verdict?" Kyros asked, entering his office.

"Sit."

"That bad." His cousin landed in the chair with a thump. "You sensed it, too, I see. The cop is an oracle."

He'd felt the magic flowing through Derek after only a minute of him arriving in the shop. Oracles could be dangerous even though they were human and not immortal. "Yes. I know."

"I wonder what lineage. Delphi? Dodona? Legadea? Eathas?"

"Doesn't matter."

"I guess not. Still, him having oracle power means fucking trouble. Just give me the word and the lawman won't be a problem for us or anyone else ever again."

As upsetting as the situation was, he couldn't stand the thought of the beautiful detective dying. "Killing isn't your style."

"It's in my wheelhouse, Titus. You know that."

He did. Kyros had worked more than a few times with two of their cousins, Cole and Daemon, on some assassinations ordered by the council. Thankfully, there hadn't been a need for such work in quite a while.

"It's in your wheelhouse, too," Kyros said.

Yes, it was, though he hadn't been sent to kill anyone since the Spanish Inquisition. Even though the evil priest on the Promethean's payroll had committed crimes against hundreds of humans and more than a few nymphs, taking the man's life had been difficult. The inquisitor had wielded the power he'd siphoned from the nature demigoddesses against him, but Titus had finally triumphed over the bastard, though at some cost.

"Murdering Detective Stone isn't necessary. The man is only doing his job. Nothing more. Besides, he doesn't know how to focus his power."

Kyros didn't seem to be convinced. "Fuck. He's got talent. Who knows how much? Since he's an oracle, we can't charm the guy either."

"True. But his power isn't stolen." He'd learned that fact during the questioning. He'd sent a tiny, invisible flicker through the detective to take stock of his abilities. As Titus expected, Stone appeared to be unaware of his own power. That was likely a good thing since skilled oracles could draw unwelcome attention from some very dark reaches. "It's natural, thankfully."

"Yes, but that doesn't mean he isn't a danger. You know as well as I that many of the oracles defected to the Public in the past." Kyros looked back at the door as if expecting a band of evil devotees to rush them. Of course, none came. His cousin turned to him. "Either way, if he starts snooping around into our affairs, we'll have to shut him down."

"Maybe so. Maybe not."

"Shit, Titus. Don't tell me you're thinking about fucking him?"

Kyros knew him too well. "Okay. I won't. Besides, he might be straight."

"He's not straight."

"You think everyone is gay." It was a game he'd played with Kyros for most of their lives. Kyros never faltered from his belief that every attractive man in the world was available to bed. Only the most unappealing males made his list of straights.

"You're playing with hellfire, Titus. It's the blackness inside him that is drawing you in, isn't it?"

"There's more to the detective than just his aura." Detective Stone had also been gorgeous. Tall and muscular, with eyes the color of rich chocolate a person could get lost in. Beautifully masculine in form, he had a square jaw and big hands. The mortal ticked off all his boxes for the perfect dream guy.

"Use your head. A little divine intervention in the love game is one thing. Murder is another." Kyros leaned forward. "Promise me you won't fuck him. Please. It's too dangerous."

"You're right." Even though Titus's pedigree included the major players in the match-making biz, he'd never personally experienced love. Lust, yes. Love, no. "Doesn't matter if I want him or not, he's on one end of this and I'm on the other."

"I'm glad you said that. Make sure you keep that in your thick head. There are a hundred gorgeous mortals just outside the shop walking up and down Cedar Springs Road. You've had your share of them these past few weeks. Pick some more. Have an orgy. I don't give a fuck. Just leave the detective alone. We can't afford you getting distracted. If it comes to us or him, you know what I will choose."

He did. "It won't come to that."

"Seriously, are we busted?" Kyros's stare was filled with concern.

Even the room seemed to sigh with worry. "No. Not yet." But he wasn't sure they would be safe for long. "We just need to stay off of the radar of the higher-ups and handle things here."

"Dad promised to help if we needed him."

"Too soon for that." Uncle Notos was the only insurance they had left. Best to not cash in on that policy until they absolutely must.

"Let's check on the customers who received one of my special tats and see how they are doing."

"Already sent half the list to your cell with contact information for them. I'll take the other half. Only seven total. We know about Barnes, so that leaves six. Three and three, so it shouldn't take us long."

"Deal." He prayed it wasn't too late. "We've got to make sure they are in good shape and not being watched. If we had more time, I'd say we could drive to each of their places, but we don't have that luxury. We'll need to teleport discretely to them. Personal visitation, understand?"

"Face to face. Check. Invisible. Check. This whole shit might only be a terrible coincidence. You know that, right?"

"I know." But he knew it might not be, too.

"Have you considered that the magic might've failed on Barnes?" His cousin wasn't much of an optimist most of the time, but for now, he was glad he was at least trying to be.

Best to keep things real, if only a little. "It didn't fail."

"Maybe. We'll see. I need a couple of bites of ambrosia before we get on this." His cousin stood. "As low as I am on energy right now, I bet I couldn't even teleport across the street. How about you? You hungry?"

"For a steak? Yes."

"You know what I mean."

"I do. Just fucking with you." He scanned his power. His divine energy was high. Odd. It had been several days since he'd eaten or drank the ambrosia, the divine food and drink they'd brought with them from home. "I'm in good shape."

His cousin shrugged. "I'm betting you'll be calling on me to come get you because you run out of juice."

He shook his head. "I won't."

"Yeah. Whatever."

"Kyros, you don't have to do this."

"Thank you, Captain." The mocking salute was typical of his cousin's way. "I'm here. I'm not leaving your side."

"If we're caught, the penalty will be very high." Likely they'd both be put out of commission for several decades, if not centuries. Their family patriarchs and matriarchs weren't known for controlling their tempers. Disobedience wasn't taken lightly. "This is my fight, not yours."

"You know I'm in. I told you that when you started this business. Don't ask me again, okay?" Kyros was loyal and wouldn't leave, not even after every possibility was tried, successful or not.

"I won't." He held out his hand. "To the bitter end."

"And beyond." Kyros smiled, taking his hand and shaking it. "Should we tell the others about this?"

Making a difference in the world was not only their dream but was also the dream of most of the young descendants of Olympus.

"Let's wait until we know more to contact them." When they did, he wanted Krystal to be the first to know. She had the uncanny gift of calming the others.

Nine immortals, all cousins, all born during the last baby boom of Olympus over two hundred years ago, had banded secretly together to rebel against the old ways. It was their birthright. It was part of their DNA to aid mortals. Several cousins had been left out of the loop of the undertaking for a variety of reasons. But the nine believed that if their effort worked, the others would join their cause. Their elders had retired, leaving their legacy on the sidelines. Titus had been the first to act, to intervene, and to follow his nature. Kyros had joined him willingly. He prayed this roadblock would be skirted and they could resume their work. For now, no more magical tats.

"Titus, before we start investigating, we better upload your next webcast. It's overdue, and the emails coming in are about to bring down the server."

"Sure thing." It was crazy but his weekly webcast already had over three thousand subscribers. Who knew an art class on tats would cause that much buzz?

5

Titus remained invisible inside the home of his former customer. Phillip had been the second human to receive a special tattoo from him. Seeing the man holding hands on the couch with his new love made his day.

The other customer he'd visited had been better than he could've imagined. Love was in the air. God, his job was amazing. Why had he waited so long to defy the family? Because of the risk to him and to them, that was why.

Kyros materialized next to him, carrying a bottle of ambrosia. Like him, he was invisible to mortal eyes. Silently, Kyros's thoughts came through, loud and clear. "I'm done. Had to drop back by the shop to get a bottle of the good stuff. Teleporting takes it out of you. Want a drink?" His cousin held the container out for him to take.

He answered silently. "No thanks. I'm in good shape. What condition did you find our customers in?"

"No issues. Looks like the misfiring tat on Barnes might've only been a fluke. What about you?"

He didn't believe the mortal's tat had misfired. "Sam Barnes's death wasn't a fluke or a suicide. I already checked on the first guy on my list. He was good. I just have one left, Paul, the guy from earlier today."

"Honey, you want something to drink?" the man next to Phillip asked.

"I can't believe I found you, Brad. You're too good to be true."

"No, you are, love. You've changed my life." The doting mortal leaned down and kissed his lover. "How about some hot tea?"

Phillip nodded. "Yes, please."

Kyros shook his head. "You might've gone a little overboard on the ink with this guy. A bit mushy if you ask me."

"But I didn't ask you."

Brad exited.

Titus scanned Phillip's aura. It was a warm gold—utter bliss. "This mortal is truly happy. That's reward enough from me." Satisfied with his handiwork, he smiled.

"Seriously, good job, cousin. You've made quite a difference in our customers' lives. How does it feel?"

"Nice. Really nice." It felt right. This was what he was born to do. "You ready to jump into this with me if we figure out who is responsible for Barnes's death?"

"Don't you mean 'once we figure' it out? I'm here and not at Olympus, aren't I?"

He treasured Kyros's loyalty, and the last thing he wanted to do was fail him. "You know what I mean. You can't imagine how wonderful it feels to influence and help mortals." His cousin deserved his own chance to experience the joy of aiding a human, making a difference in someone's life.

"Be careful, Titus. Don't get addicted." Kyros's caution was warranted.

"I won't. When we prove the last guy on my list is okay, then we can work on solving Barnes's murder." *No way it was suicide.*

"Do you want me to take the last one?" Kyros asked.

"No. I've got it."

"We still have to deal with Detective Stone. He doesn't strike me as a man who ever lets well enough alone. Remember how he was about getting my mom's address. He's not stupid, which is a big problem for us. Charming him won't work since he's an oracle. We might have to talk to Cole or Daemon for a favor."

A protective rage for Derek rolled through him. "We're not killing him, Kyros. That's final." Hot white energy shot out of his fingertips and swirled around him.

"Fuck. Cool it, Titus. I'm not your enemy."

"Sorry." Reining in his power, he was surprised how strong and sudden his reaction was to Kyros's deadly suggestion on how to handle the detective.

"That was quite an impressive display of divine fire, cousin."

He shrugged.

"Damn. You're still juiced up to the brim even after teleporting twice?"

He scanned himself and felt the intense power within. How? "This doesn't make sense."

"Maybe it has something to do with you being the new demigod of love and all."

"I'm not. I don't have worshipers. I don't have a temple. I have customers, and only a few of those. They couldn't give me enough adoration to be of consequence."

"Maybe not, but you explain why your tank is barely down a drop. Keep this up and you might even become a full-blown god. That would be a kick in the teeth to the elders."

"I'm not here to build a following. You know that." The elders wouldn't ever allow him—or anyone else for that matter—to attempt something so risky. Keeping humanity in the dark about their existence was priority number one for the counsel. Until he knew what or who had been behind Barnes's death, he would side with their judgment.

"I know. I remember the lessons. It's too dangerous, addictive. Power can be quite seductive."

Brad came back into the room. "Here's your tea, sweetheart." He handed Phillip a cup.

"Thank you, doll," their former customer said.

"Kyros, we're not killing Derek."

"Remember Prometheus? He gave the humans the benefit of the doubt, too. "

Of course he knew. All immortals knew. Prometheus's followers had twisted the stories of his abduction to the masses, saying Zeus had punished him for taking fire to humankind. Even to this very day, that early propaganda was taught in schools and universities.

"Of course, but we don't have to kill Derek. He's innocent."

"Hardly innocent, but we'll do this your way, cousin. The detective lives until we have no other options." Kyros patted him on the shoulder. "We'll figure this out together. There's got to be a loophole or some fact we're missing." Then his cousin dematerialized in a flash of green light.

"Did you feel that?" His former customer asked Brad.

"Feel what?"

"I think someone is watching us," Phillip said. As if to punctuate the fact that mortals could be dangerous and unpredictable, the human with his magical tat turned his direction.

Without hesitating, he flashed out and to the home of the last of his customers he needed to visit.

WALKING into a stranger's home was commonplace for Derek, especially since this house contained two dead bodies. Commonplace or not, he wasn't at ease being here. His curse was seizing his thoughts, forcing him to feel things, to know things others couldn't. Just like it had done at the morgue earlier,

He and Michael walked past the crime scene techs to the bedroom where the two naked guys were.

"What are we looking at, Kincel?" he asked the lead of the crime scene team.

"Place is clean except for this." The officer held up a bag filled with white powder. "Looks like these two partied a little too hard. This is really pure shit, too."

"You think they were dealing?" Michael asked Kincel.

He shrugged. "I just gather the evidence, Vende. You and Stone here make the conclusions."

Derek looked around the space. It didn't scream dealer to him. "Did they both live here?"

"Nope," the officer stated. "The guy on the floor works at a coffee shop and lives with his sister off Hall Street in a condo. He'd left word with her where he was. Apparently, these two had quite the whirlwind romance in the last few hours."

"A random fuck gone awry with too much coke," Michael said. "Open and shut."

But Derek wasn't buying it. He could feel the energy in the air. It vibrated fast and hot. This wasn't some afternoon quickie for these two vics. They had cared for each other very much. There was something else he was picking up on. Out of the corner of his eye, he saw Titus, the owner of the tattoo shop, standing to his left by the window.

"What the fuck are you doing here?" he asked, turning Love's direction. But the man wasn't there.

"Who are you talking to, Stone?" Kincel asked.

"His spirit guides, I bet," Michael mocked.

A few of the techs laughed. He didn't give them the pleasure of responding though he cursed his mother's gift and pushed it deep down as best he could. Feelings could go fuck themselves. He wanted facts. Only facts.

"How long have they been dead?" he asked.

"Not long. The sister freaked when her brother's boss called saying the vic had never returned after taking a break. She's the mayor's daughter's best friend. So you know the drill. Protocol went out the window. Search warrant got rushed and issued with a little arm twisting, and voilà, here we are. We got the call about five o'clock."

"Send us what you have to the unit. I think we can turn this around ASAP. This isn't a double homicide. You agree, Stone?"

He was about to nod but didn't because of what he saw on the ankle of one of the vics.

"No. I don't agree, Vende."

"Don't fuck with me any more today. I swear I'll rip you apart if you do."

Derek stepped closer to the bed. "See this," he said, pointing to the ink. "This exact tattoo was on Barnes."

Michael moved next to him and leaned down. "Shit. You're right."

"Coincidence?" Kincel asked.

Derek shook his head. This one had some residual power left in it, just like Barnes's had. He sensed that it had been brimming with more energy before whoever had murdered these two had stripped it away. *Supernatural shit. Fuck.* "There's no such thing as coincidence in our line of work, officer."

"Does the other guy have a tat like this one?" Michael asked Kincel.

"Nope. No tats at all," the lead answered.

Michael sighed. "Looks like you were right about Barnes, Stone."

"We'll see." He couldn't help but look back at the space where he'd thought he'd seen Titus standing. He hadn't been able to get the sexy man out of his thoughts since meeting him at Love Ink. Perhaps that was why his imagination had placed him at this crime scene, but he didn't think so. How much the gorgeous owner of the tat shop was wrapped up in this case he wasn't sure. Still, his mother's wretched gift clanged inside his head over and over with one clear message.

Titus is in trouble.

6

Titus teleported back to Love Ink and found Kyros about to open the door to a woman on the other side of the glass. His muscles tightened at the fucked-up mess he'd just left.

"She might've seen you, cousin. What were you thinking materializing in the open?" Kyros asked. "Even I had the sense to do it in your office, out of view of the windows."

"The mortal female didn't see me." He'd flashed back to the shop without thinking after realizing Derek had actually penetrated through his invisibility magic. "You can't work on her."

"She has an appointment."

"Doesn't matter." Paul was dead because of him, and Derek had seen him. "We're done."

Kyros held up his hand. "Okay. I take it you found our last customer and didn't like what you saw."

"You could say that again."

"I'll tell the human to get lost and then you have to fill me in."

"Exactly what I planned to do." His family, the gods had been exposed. After years of seclusion and hiding, he'd brought danger to his loved ones by opening up his business in Dallas. What a fool he'd been, believing his deception would never get out.

After Kyros sent the woman on her way, he came back. "I didn't have to invoke a charm on her, cousin, only had to promise to meet her for coffee. Silly mortal, my tastes are for satyrs, not nymphs."

"Cut the crap. We're in big trouble." Titus's heart ripped in two knowing Derek would no longer be safe once the elders got wind of what was going on here. It was as if a sharp dagger had been shoved into his chest.

"What did you find, cousin?"

"Paul Crane is dead."

"Fuck. You think this is the work of Prometheans?" Kyros asked.

"Could be." With enough of a stolen god's power, the most devout could work horrible miracles. Killing didn't require much.

"You better be wrong about this. It's been hard enough to keep our venture a secret from the family. If we have followers of Prometheus sneaking around, we are completely fucked. Hell, even Zeus, as powerful as he was back then, knew it was best to pull away from humankind after Prometheus's kidnapping by his high priest. How did they find us?"

"I don't know, but we need to fix this. That means we must find out who or what is behind these killings."

"How are we going to keep this from Olympus, cousin? And more importantly, how do we start cleaning up this disaster?"

"We're going to shut down the business. I should have never come here and tried this."

"Titus, don't say that. You're our only hope for a different life."

By *our*, his cousin meant him and Titus and the other young demigods and demigoddesses, especially Cole, Lukus, Daemon, Atreus, Zil, Jayson, and Krystal. They were as different from one another as could be except for one thing—they all wanted to impact humanity. Secretly, they'd discussed just that for many decades, but none had taken the risk until him.

He looked at his cousin and shook his head. "I shouldn't have done this. It was a mistake."

A flash of blue filled the room, and a wet hot wind swirled tighter and tighter into a sphere of gray and lightning. When it stopped spinning, Kyros's dad, Uncle Notos materialized, wearing a dark suit and red tie. "You screwed up, boys. That's for sure. I shouldn't have encouraged you. It's my fault. Two dead humans with divine tats on their flesh, empty of their power."

Kyros asked, "Father, do the elders know?"

"Unfortunately, yes. Zeus was on the golf course when one of his spies, a siren, came to him with the news. Apparently, she's a dispatcher for the Dallas Police Department." Kyros's dad, god of the South Wind, sat in one of the chairs. "We best get started cleaning up this mess before we have to face the council. That's why I was sent here."

Titus looked in the eyes of the god and felt a heavy guilt hit him in the center of his gut. "I'm sorry, Uncle Notos. I'm the one at fault, not you."

"Let Zeus and the others decide who is to blame. I'm sure we will all be punished in some fashion, but there's work to be done. How many mortals did you place your mark on?"

"Seven," he answered.

"Five are fine. We saw them today," Kyros added.

"Good job," Uncle Notos said. "What's your next step?"

It pained him to his very core, but he knew what he had to do. "Closing the shop."

"True. You know the law. You will also have to eliminate any humans too close to the truth," the older god said.

Titus couldn't bear the thought of Derek being dead. "I don't believe there's anyone who will be a threat to the family, Uncle Notos."

"Really? I doubt that. At the very least there's a killer we need to find. If he is working for the Order he might lead us to the Prometheans and then to our lost brother."

"Prometheus?" Kyros asked his dad.

"Exactly, son."

Titus couldn't imagine the hell the god must've suffered all those millennia. "You surely don't think he's still alive?"

Uncle Notos answered, "I believe he is."

The thought of being imprisoned by the Prometheans so long was horrifying to him. He hoped the ancient god suffered no more. "What now?"

"Boys, let's make a plan."

More than an hour later, the steps were set. Kyros and Uncle Notos left him alone at Love Ink.

Kyros was drafting some of their cousins to help. Some would search for the killer and find out if he was a Promethean. Others would become invisible bodyguards for their five surviving customers until the murderer was found.

Uncle Notos had left to deal with the family, especially Zeus, to buy them more time to finish the cleanup in Dallas. If they succeeded, their punishment might be lessened.

Titus's task was clear, but definitely not simple, troubling him beyond measure. Besides closing up shop, he had to find out what the police—and in particular, Detective Stone—knew. If any were too close to the truth that would expose the gods, his clear responsibility was to wipe critical details from their minds and to kill the one mortal whose thoughts he couldn't erase. That was his duty. Even though he'd killed before, he couldn't bear thinking about taking Derek's last breath, seeing his eyes glaze over, feeling his pulse stop.

"Why am I feeling so strongly about Derek? I only just met him."

A male voice he knew well resounded in his mind. "You're a demigod of love, Titus. Our bloodline feels deeply. This mortal means something to you."

"Where are you Cupid?" His guilt rose up like a volcano. He'd stolen his grandfather's arrow to make the ink of love.

"Here I am, boy." The ancient god materialized softly—no flashing lights or smoke—in front of him, and by his side was his wife, Titus's grandmother, Psyche. "I'm not a fan of my Roman name, grandson. Call me Eros or grandfather, though I prefer the later from you."

Unlike the chubby infant the Italians used when depicting Eros in their art, his granddad appeared as a young, winged man. Replace the jeans and dark shirt he was wearing with a white robe and most mortals would've thought him an angel. Titus's grandmother, too, had her own wings, though unlike her husband's white feathers, hers were multicolored like a butterfly's. Her blonde curls fell to her shoulders. Her choice of dress was simple yet elegant. The pale green blouse made her eyes shine even brighter.

"I'm sorry for what I've done," he said, lowering his gaze to the floor. "I'm guilty. I stole one of your arrows to make my magic ink."

"Look at us," his grandmother commanded.

He obeyed her. Gone were their wings. To any mortal that might pass the windows of Love Ink, his grandparents would seem like a typical young couple, though more attractive than most.

"That's my boy," she said, waving her hand. A shimmer of power filled the room. "That should hinder any unwanted eavesdroppers. You've got more on your plate than any young immortal should have to deal with, Titus. Zeus's ridiculous laws need to be broken."

"Darling, they aren't Zeus's laws. They are the council's," Eros pointed out.

"Poppycock. Expecting demigods to deny their very nature is contemptible. How many times have you bemoaned to me about your suffering? You miss the old days. Don't deny it. Aiding human passion is part of you."

"Grandmother, it's too dangerous. Three mortals are dead because of my actions."

Psyche gave him a hug. "Not true, sweetie. Humans are responsible for this. Remember, I was mortal once."

He nodded, recalling the story about how her and his grandfather's relationship began. "Let me get your arrow and give it back to you, grandfather."

"Keep it, Titus. It's yours."

"That's why I love you," his grandmother said, kissing Eros on the cheek. "Grandson, tell us about this detective fellow."

"You dare to call me a meddler, sweetheart." His grandfather shook his head. "You might want to take a long look in the mirror."

"Hush. Let the boy talk."

Titus sighed, and then began. "He's an oracle, a descendant."

"I understand," Psyche said. "The man's mind is impervious to charm or influence."

"Hopefully the oracle bloodline is thin in him so his gifts are weak," his grandfather added.

"Uncle Notos and Kyros are counting on me to kill Derek. They didn't say it, but it is my duty, and I could see the expectation on their faces before they left."

"Hermes's son-in-law and grandson might need a kick in the butt from me," Psyche snapped.

Eros touched her cheek. "Darling, the boy is right. It is the law."

She jerked away. "I already said it is an idiotic law. Did you not hear me? If you and I had followed the law of the family, we wouldn't be together now. Your mother had gotten all of the old guard on her side when you and I got together. Remember?"

"I do."

"She was a monster, Eros."

His grandfather looked up to the ceiling. "Don't speak of Aphrodite like that, honey. You never know who might be listening."

"I protected the room from eavesdroppers. Besides, it's true."

Eros cupped his wife's chin. "Maybe so, but you and Mom have overcome a lot over the years."

Titus loved that his grandparents were so close. Would he ever experience such intimacy and trust with someone like the handsome detective?

"We have. That's true. Enough talk about the past. We're here to help our grandson, husband. He's found his one true love."

Titus's jaw dropped. "I have? Derek? I barely know him."

Eros shrugged. "Doesn't matter when it comes to the heart. You've only been in the love game a few weeks to my several millennia. Trust me. He's your one."

"You felt it the second you met him, I bet," Psyche said.

"I guess so."

"Same for me and your granddad when we first stumbled into each other. Love is the most powerful force in the world, despite what Zeus and the others say."

"She's right, grandson," Eros said with a wink.

"But what if Derek is part of this? What if he's tied up with the Prometheans?" He hated to think that was a possibility, but he must. "Then what can I do?"

Psyche was about to speak, but Eros stopped her with a raised hand. "No, love. If this detective is working for the Prometheans, whether willingly or unwillingly, he must die. None of us would be safe. Not even our grandson."

"But the oracle is his true love." Her voice was so tender and soft, breaking Titus's heart.

"I know. I pray the mortal is pure." His grandfather turned back to him. "You need to be sure, grandson. Really sure."

"Yes. I do."

His grandfather looked him straight in the eyes. "If the detective is in league with the Prometheans, I'll talk to my father about sending some of his invisible soldiers to finish the job so you won't have to."

"I don't want Ares involved." His shoulders tightened. "I'll do my duty if it comes to that."

"He's approaching," Eros stated.

"Who?" he asked. A knock on the locked entrance door pulled him from his thoughts.

"Your detective is here," Psyche answered.

DEREK LOOKED through the glass at the man whose image he couldn't seem to get out of his head ever since meeting him. The door to Love Ink was locked, which was strange since it was only seven thirty. The business hours printed on the door indicated it should be open.

Titus left the young couple he'd been talking to and unlocked and opened the door. "Hello, Detective. Please, come in."

"Thank you." He stepped past Titus and looked at the pair already in the building. "Customers?"

"Family. Cousins."

Derek's curse told him the first word had been truthful but the

last had been a lie. Everything about Titus didn't make any sense.
Derek looked at the young couple and felt utterly drawn to them. His
extra senses were exploding like fireworks about these two.

"Hello. I'm Detective Stone."

The woman smiled broadly. "Yes, you are." She left the embrace
of her young man and headed straight to him. Her steps were
graceful and full of life. "You're perfect, Detective."

Before he could stop her, the young beauty put her arms around
him and squeezed. At first he tensed and almost shoved her away, but
something about her embrace was so innocent and caring, he
stopped himself. And then it hit him. *She's not human, at least not
completely.* What the hell was she then?

"My love, let the detective be," her companion said.

"Everything is going to be just fine." She giggled, released him,
and stepped back a couple of feet. "I'm sure he's trustworthy, Eros."

Eros? His fact-finding into the tat had uncovered that name.
"You're Mr. Love's cousins?"

"Yes, we are," the male answered.

Another lie.

He tried to shove his sixth sense down. What his curse was
shouting in his mind about these two supposed cousins of Titus was
completely ridiculous and totally illogical. Was it finally time for
the guys in white coats to take him away? His research on the
symbol of the three circles and arrow had gotten a hit on the
Internet on Greek and Roman mythology. That had to be the cause
of Derek's imagination getting the better of him. "Eros is an unusual
name."

"Not where I come from, Officer." The man's tone sharpened. "We
need to get home, my love."

He turned to the beauty. "Don't tell me your name is Psyche?"

"That's about enough," Eros snapped and the air vibrated with
something unseen but quite dangerous.

"Hush, husband," the woman said. "Yes, Detective. I am Psyche.
Our family is enamored with Greek myths. You know some about
such things yourself, don't you?"

"A little," he confessed. "This case required that I look deeper into it."

Eros stepped protectively between Psyche and him. "It was nice meeting you, Detective. If you don't mind, we have things to attend to."

This is the god of Love. The truth shimmered on Derek's skin. The name of the business and Titus's last name were all starting to make sense in the craziest way. "Sure thing. Nice to meet you two."

His world was turning upside down and sideways. Was the invisible realm his mother so longed for even more real than she'd believed? If so, how the hell was he going to deal with that?

The god's shoulders dropped a fraction. Disaster averted —for now.

"Titus, we're staying in town. If you need us, just call," Eros said.

"I will. I promise."

Psyche stepped around her husband and kissed Derek on the cheek, sending a spark through his body. "It was nice to meet you, Detective. Very nice indeed."

"Thank you. I hope we meet again."

"It's a deal," she said.

The couple exited the shop, leaving him alone with Titus, who was clearly related to them. What did that make him?

"You've been studying mythology because of Barnes's murder?" Love asked.

"And Crane's, another customer of yours." Why was he imaging what his one and only suspect would look like naked? He needed to keep focused.

"What happened to him, Derek?"

"I think you already know." He recalled seeing the image of Titus for a split-second at the victim's home. He'd dismissed it the best he could then. But now, the possibility that Love was there using some kind of divine magic might prove true. *I'm really going to go there— believing in gods and goddesses?*

"Tell me, Detective."

"He's dead," he told him flatly. His mind was spinning. What was it about this man that made him feel less in control, more unsteady and unsure? Clearly his emotions were running things, not logic. *Get a grip, Derek.* "Double homicide, though like Barnes, made to look like a suicide."

"Is that why you're here? To question me?"

Yes, that was the reason. Vende was already working on getting a warrant for Titus, but the evidence was likely too thin to get the green light to bring him in. That was why he was really here. To try to uncover any other shred of a clue that might lead them to an arrest and then finally to a conviction. His abominable gift roared inside him like a lion on a rampage. Rarely did he sense the future, like he was now. If he didn't veer from this path, both he and Titus would die. He could see it clearly in his mind's eye.

"I'm here to get a tattoo from you." Where did that come from? He hadn't planned on getting a tattoo.

"We're no longer in business. I'm closing Love Ink."

"You know that makes you look more guilty, don't you?" Two men were dead. Love was involved in some way. That's why Derek had come here. That was the only reason. If he let Titus draw the symbol on his flesh, would he be able to follow through until he uncovered all of Love's secrets? What then? Arresting a child of the gods couldn't end well. Not for either of them.

Titus shrugged. "Can't be helped."

"Okay. Your call. But I want one of your tattoos. The same one you put on Barnes and Crane."

"That's a bit morbid, Detective."

"Not morbid at all. I read up on everything that there is to know about that symbol."

Titus's eyebrows rose. "And?"

"It's quite old. It was discovered on the walls of a tomb in the ancient Greek city of Thespiae in the eighteen hundreds. Some believe it has to do with the god of Love, since he was the one most revered there. Like most symbols of that time, it probably had some kind of mystical significance."

"And you want me to put this symbol on you?"

He had to reconsider what he was requesting. If his heightened senses were right and Titus was a member of a mythical race, the symbol might have the power to open up ones heart to experience love.

Love? It was nothing more than chemicals interacting inside the body creating something akin to illness and insanity. A person's heart beat faster. Their knees weakened and they often became tongue-tied. Thoughts were difficult to understand or voice.

He hadn't felt those emotions in a very long time, not since kicking Bill out of his home. Was it crazy to want them again? Of course it was.

"I want you to give me my first tattoo, Titus. I want the symbol of love. Will you give it to me or not?"

The gorgeous creature sighed. "Okay. I'll do it. You'll be my last customer, Derek."

7

Titus finished the work on the symbol on Derek's left pec, just above his pierced nipple. Seeing the body jewelry on the detective had been a nice surprise. Perhaps the uptight lawman wasn't so uptight after all. "All done."

He'd thought about using the enchanted ink on the desirable human, but then he'd changed his mind being unsure what impact it might have on the detective. Considering his unique bloodline too many variables existed to take that risk. Had that been a mistake? If the well-built oracle was in league with the Prometheans, a spelled tattoo might've produced an advantage he needed over him.

Gazing into the man's eyes, he just couldn't believe Derek could ever be his enemy. Was that just wishful thinking on his part? And what if the detective was *the one* as his grandparents had suspected? The only way to know now was to take the muscular mortal to bed. But he couldn't indulge himself, no matter what his grandparents believed. Duty demanded he tread carefully around his last customer. Realizing Derek would be the final human to sit in his chair for a tattoo ripped his heart apart. His dream to intercede for humankind was over. Love Ink would be no more. Two humans were dead and the family might be in terrible danger because of what he'd done.

"Thank you," Derek said, peering down at his new artwork. "It looks great."

"Anything else I can do for you?" he asked.

"Just this." The detective leaned forward and shocked him with a steamy, powerful kiss. The mortal's full lips pressed hard against his mouth, causing his body's temperature to warm.

When Derek released him, Titus looked directly in his eyes. "You're gay?"

He nodded.

"And you thought I was too because...?" he asked to try to throw him off.

"I-I assumed you were." The sweet human's worried look was thrilling and enticing.

"You know what they say about the word 'assume,' don't you? It makes an 'ass' out of 'u' and 'me.'"

Derek shook his head and closed his eyes. "Your shop is on Cedar Springs. This is the gay area. Umm." He opened his eyes and fixed him with a gaze that reached deep inside his very soul. "I don't know what to say, Titus."

Even though keeping Derek in the dark might've been the best strategy, he just couldn't bear seeing him suffer. "I'm gay. I was just fucking with you, Detective."

"That's a relief," he said with a sigh. Once again, Derek planted a kiss on him.

The sudden change in the mortal was puzzling. Even though the ink on his chest was absolutely normal, Derek's abrupt turnaround from hardened accuser to unrelenting seducer indicated something divine might be at work. Had his grandfather sent one of his invisible arrows through the detective's heart when Titus wasn't looking? No. He would've sensed that. Then what had invoked this U-turn in the oracle?

When the beautiful creature's tongue thrust out, he parted his own lips slightly, granting him an intimate entrance. Inhaling Derek's masculine scent with its subtle notes of leather and rain melted him completely. For now, his urges were in the driver's seat. Duty would have to wait for later to make room for what he wanted, what he craved. His uncontrollable hunger spurred him forward.

He wrapped his arms around Derek's waist and pulled him in tight. The potent human's breathy moan shot into him, causing his dick to expand. His pulse felt like fire, burning him inside as the red-blooded detective continued to harness his mouth with a wicked wet lip-lock. He'd never been kissed like this before by anyone, mortal or immortal.

When the delicious human finally ended their kiss, Titus gasped for air, overcome with a flood of emotions and sensations racing through his mind and body.

"I thought it best to get that out of the way." The oracle's choco-late-colored eyes were filled with lust and temptation.

He pulled Derek in even closer. "I'm glad you did. You're a terrific kisser."

"So are you. God, your body is amazing. I'm not wearing a shirt. Neither should you." The man who might be the biggest threat to the family in many years snaked his hands under Titus's T-shirt.

"You were getting a tattoo, detective. I wasn't."

"That's a poor excuse, if you ask me." The feel of Derek's finger-tips on his skin, rubbing up and down his torso, made his flesh burn deliciously. "You must live at the gym, Titus."

"I work out some, but it's mostly genetics, I believe."

"I bet your DNA is quite remarkable."

"What do you mean by that?" he asked.

"I'm nuts for your body, but I think I would rather show you than tell you. Let me start by helping you take off your T-shirt." Without another word, Derek pulled the garment off of him. Tossing it to the floor, the dauntless human began kissing his nipples, tenderly at first, and then with each pass from one to the other the intensity grew more urgent and demanding. Derek's lips tightened on his bits of taut flesh, drawing him in deeper and deeper.

Titus spread his fingers wide, trying to feel more of the delicious man's skin all at once. Derek's shoulders were rock solid. Slowly, as the oracle moistened and tortured his tits, he sent his hands down the sexy man's back. Even this part of Derek's body raised his desires to an insane level. He'd never wanted anyone like he wanted him right now, right here.

A couple walked by the big window at the front of the shop but thankfully didn't peer their direction.

"Derek, since I don't have blinds on my windows or the entrance door, we better take this to my office. I don't think either of us wants to get turned into the police for indecent exposure."

The unflinching beast sucked hard on his tits, making him dizzy with desire. "I've got a badge, sweetheart. Besides, I want to have you in every indecent way possible." Derek's left hand went down between Titus's legs until the only thing between the mortal's finger-tips and his cock was cotton. "I want to taste you, Mr. Love. Taste and swallow you. I want to feel every inch of your muscled frame next to mine. I want to be in you, and I want you to be in me. That indecent enough for you?" His wink spoke volumes more than his wicked words had.

He struggled to catch his breath. "Are you drunk or high? You don't seem like yourself to me."

Like a victorious barbarian, Derek laughed. "We've only known each other for a blink of an eye, but I'm more myself than I've been in a very long time, thanks to you. You want to continue this in your office? I'm fine with that as long as you lose your clothes, sweetheart."

By the primordial gods, this man knew how to enflame him. "Yes. I promise. Now, let's go before we get busted."

Derek leapt to his feet and kissed him on the lips again. "You've got a deal, Titus." He walked to the hallway that led to the office, kicking off his shoes and removing his clothing in the sexiest strip-tease ever.

By the time the mortal was at the other end of the passage next to the door, Titus's cock had lengthened to its full nine and a half inches, causing him more than a little discomfort.

"Coming, Mr. Love?" Derek's seductive tone sent a rush of heat and want through him.

"You bet your gorgeous ass I am."

DEREK STEPPED into Titus's office and leaned against the front of the desk. His one and only suspect entered without a stitch of clothing on as promised. "The hallway must look like the closet floor of a teenager."

"It does indeed," the handsome fiend said.

He'd always been attracted to manly men, and Titus definitely fit the bill. Masculinity gushed out of him like a geyser. He had the very essence of manhood. A man's man.

"I like a guy who keeps his word." His mind swirled with unleashed passions, clearly the result of the magical symbol on his chest. He was free to feel, to be, to enjoy this sexy beast.

"Me, too." Titus's multicolored eyes still transfixed him. In them he could see loyalty, goodness, and more. His muscled arms and chest were sights to behold. And six-packs and eight-packs be damned, the brute's midsection was a shredded masterpiece. Even his cock was a thing of beauty. Thick. Long. Monstrous. Pointing straight up to heaven. The patch of trimmed pubic hair only accentuated how well formed and how perfect every inch and every detail of him was.

The truth was he'd wanted to be with Titus the moment he'd seen him. The little time he'd spent with him, gotten to know him, the cravings to bed the dazzling man had only gotten worse. Now with the new ink on his skin, the urges were uncontainable. Sure, he'd asked Titus for the tat. He would like to be able to blame his fall on someone or something else, but he couldn't. It wasn't because of his mother's curse or a sudden bout of insanity, or anything else.

The fault was his alone. Now, that the ink was part of him, he surrendered to its power.

"Come here then, Mr. Love."

"It's Titus. Remember?"

"Titus, then. Come closer."

As the unblemished man stepped closer, Derek dropped to his knees. "Your cock is massive." He wrapped Titus's thick shaft with his right hand, and cupped his heavy balls with his left.

Big manly fingers grabbed him by the shoulders. "Yours could be mine's twin. It's a beast, too. Let me guess. Nine and a half?"

"Too bad the carnival folks only guess age and weight, Titus. You'd be top dog as a dick-length predictor. Still, I think you're a bit thicker than me. Let me check." Derek licked the head of Titus's dick, savoring the salty slickness oozing from the slit. Squeezing his balls, he opened his mouth wide and dove down the substantial cock until it hit the back of his throat. *My god, he's big.* The tension and excitement ramped up inside him as he sucked until his cheeks hollowed out. Need scraped every cell in his body. He thirsted for Love's hot liquid, hoping to drown in every drop.

When he felt the captivating devil's hands on the back of his head, pulling him in tighter, he shoved his hand down to his own cock and began pumping away.

"Derek, no. Don't come."

Instantly, he obeyed. His yearning to please Titus was so present and so consuming inside him.

"I want to taste you, too." Love's words were deep and breathy, full of lust. "After—"

"Shh. I'm glad. You'll get to, too." Having this man's beautiful lips on his dick was something he wanted in the worst way. "Let me work my magic on you and finish what I've started."

Like a hungry wolf, he devoured every inch of Titus's cock, down his throat, deeper and deeper. Giving head had never been something he'd enjoyed before, not until now, not until Love. Up and down his dick he bobbed with his lips and fist while squeezing his meaty balls at the same time.

"God, Derek. Your mouth feels so...so...so...very *good.*"

Titus's words worked to stir him more. Irrational and loving it, he sucked like he'd never sucked before.

"*Fuck,*" Love shouted, shooting a creamy load down his throat.

He drank the beast's hot elixir, relishing every jerk, splash, and pulse of the thick cock in his mouth. Not a single drip spilled from his lips, though the quantity the devil produced was considerable.

After Titus's climax ended, he gave his thick cock one last torturous strong suck. The shiver he felt from the man thrilled him.

"Enough, Derek." Love's big hands tugged at his hair, urging him to his feet.

When they were face to face, the delicious renegade leaned in and pressed his full manly lips to his mouth. The staggering kiss liquefied every part of Derek. The merging of their mouths was fierce and impassioned. Never before had he felt like he belonged to anyone. His ex had never impacted him this way. Was this love? No. He didn't believe in such things. Maybe the tat's magic was messing with his head, his will, his logic. Maybe.

As Titus deepened their kiss, sweeping his wet tongue into Derek's mouth, his mind drifted into a dreamy, blissful space. He imagined a future with this man—a real future. He could finally see himself taking steps into a *real* relationship built on honesty and mutual respect, and not some silly emotion called love. Of course they'd need more time together, for sure, but what they would end up with would be well worth the effort, however long it took. Love's self-assurance, tenderness, and unselfishness were traits he couldn't resist.

The sweet savage peeled his lips free from him and then dropped to his knees. "My turn to pleasure you, baby."

He loved that he called him *baby*. Anyone else, he would've punched in the face. But not Titus. The savory beauty's words actually warmed him to the core.

Feeling Titus's tongue bathe his cock and balls sent gratifying jolts throughout his body. Every lick ignited more and more sensations inside him. When the dear tattoo artist gobbled up all of his cock, he clutched the man's thick dark locks and held on for dear life.

"Oh my god, your mouth feels fucking awesome."

When Titus grabbed his ass with his big thick hands, Derek was awash with a rush of anticipation. His entire body tensed as his balls began to ache. The sweet savage swallowed every inch of his dick. Then Titus's wicked lips slid back up the full length of his shaft. Down again, sucking and sucking. Slithering back up. And down. Over and over. Tiny ripples danced over his skin as the beast's oral torture sent him to the brink of a pure, wonderful madness.

Suddenly, Love released his dick and looked up at him. "You like, Derek?"

Unable to vocalize a single syllable, he nodded.

"Fuck my mouth, baby. Fuck my mouth with your beautiful cock." Titus went back to work on tormenting his dick.

Taking hold of the back of Titus's head, he pulled him in tight. "I'm inside you, sweetheart. Swallow all of me."

Titus's mastery at giving oral pleasure caused his cock to swell even more. Suddenly, he could feel a thick finger rubbing against the entrance to his ass, fueling his frenzy. Delirious and uncontrolled, Derek thrust his shooting cock deep into the handsome man's tight throat. When the stud sent a meaty digit into Derek's ass, his balls unloaded, sending his seed up his shaft and into a very greedy mouth.

After the final drop was shot, he released his hold of Titus's head. His new lover stood and fixed his stare on him. Derek hadn't let himself dream of being with anyone. A few one-time tricks here and there had been all he'd known since Bill. Being with Titus, here and now, Derek realized for the very first time that what he'd felt for Bill hadn't been love. Not even close. At its best it had been an unhealthy infatuation. He'd only known Titus for less than a day and already he had more feelings for him than he'd ever had with anyone, including his ex. He wasn't ready to call this emotion love, but it was certainly powerful and overwhelming.

Titus smiled, sending him to the stratosphere. "I'm going to kiss you, baby. I'm going to kiss you until your lips are raw and swollen."

When his lover's lips landed on his, he closed his eyes. And then something strange happened. His mother's curse went into overdrive. There was no doubt about it. It was as if he was being transported to another place, another time. The future.

A spot appeared at the back of his mind. It grew bigger and bigger, changing color with each advance. Then it morphed into a mini-movie of sorts. An image of Titus materialized in this dream. The owner of Love Ink was in a strange bedroom, kneeling down on the bed by someone. Who? Derek wanted to see, wanted to know. Willing his conscious closer, he peered down at the corpse. The empty eyes were Derek's own. He was the dead man Titus knelt beside.

The image vanished as the kiss ended.

Derek opened his eyes and looked at the man who had stolen his heart and would one day end his life.

8

———

Titus stared out the window of the shop at the heavy raindrops falling from the early morning sky. A summer shower in Dallas was a rare but welcome occurrence which normally lifted his spirits. Not now. Not today. Not after Derek's sudden exit last night.

"Are you nuts?" Kyros asked. "You let him go."

"He's not a Promethean."

His cousin glared at him. "I see. You know that because why exactly?"

"The detective isn't our enemy," he replied. "Prometheans have great faith. He has none." Derek's aura had lightened during their lovemaking, but just before leaving, the mortal's darkness deepened to the blackest black. Hopelessness.

"Did you fuck him?" Kyros asked.

"None of your damn business."

"I knew it. Fuck, Titus. Can't you keep your dick in your pants until this shit is cleaned up?"

"Of course." After Derek's exit, he thought it would be easy to do. Having multiple lovers—one, two, and three a night—had been his norm, but now he couldn't imagine being with anyone other than Derek. "Have you heard from your dad?"

"No. What about your mom?"

Titus's mother, Hedone, the Goddess of Pleasure had become more and more reclusive, rarely leaving the ranch in West Texas she and his dad, Pronomos, operated. "No."

"Maybe that's a good thing. I'm sure Uncle Pronomos is out of the loop."

That was quite the understatement. The ranch was way off the beaten path. No one just stumbled onto it. "Our granddad is still pissed at him for missing the annual Olympian celebration."

"Hermes can hold a grudge. That's for sure."

Kyros and Titus shared lineage with the god the Romans had called Mercury. He'd fathered his dad, Pronomos the satyr and Kyros's mother, Angelia, Demigoddess of Tidings.

The back of his neck suddenly began to tingle. An immortal was coming.

Black smoke materialized by the marble statue of the men embracing, and out of it came Daemon, their cousin and the grandson of Hades, carrying an ivory walking cane. He wore all white —a leather duster that came down to his calves, tight fitting jeans, polo shirt, and even his shoes were white.

Kyros glared at their guest. "For a demigod of death, you look to be dressed in the wrong color, cousin. I miss your Goth phase. Much more appropriate."

"Who says that white isn't the new Goth color of this decade? It's all about how you carry yourself. For instance, this cane has a skull on its handle. See." He held it out in front of him, obviously for them to inspect better. Then Daemon flipped it around and brought the razor-sharp point of the tip to Kyros's neck. "Goth enough for you?"

"Put that thing down before I shove it up your ass, cousin," Kyros growled.

He shrugged and brought the bottom of the cane back to the floor. "Just making my point that attitude is what makes the clothes."

Daemon was right. White suited him. In an odd sort of way, it made the dark demigod look even more sinister.

"Don't fuck with us, Daemon," Kyros snapped. "We're in no mood for it."

Hades's favorite grandson sighed. "Always so serious?"

"Only when I need to be."

"I can't believe you stole this from your mother's place, Titus," Daemon said, patting the sculpture. "Beautiful, though forgive me for saying, cousin, the story this marble tells is completely fictional. Love never lasts. No offense."

"What are you doing here?" Titus asked him.

"A little bird told me that you and Kyros have made a complete mess of things here."

"And you came to help us out, or are you only here to protect your interests?" Kyros's tone deepened to a growl.

"Hold on," Daemon said. "These were *our* interests, *our* plans. Secret plans. Now, Zeus and the entire council know Titus's violations. So fill me in."

Jayson, the grandson of Aphrodite, materialized to the left of Daemon. "Wait. The others are coming, too." He wore boots, jeans, and a leather vest but no shirt, exposing his muscled chest.

By *others*, Jayson obviously meant the cousins who had been in the know about Love Ink and all it represented.

Kyros smiled. "Left the motorcycle at home, Jayson?"

"I'm low on the juice, cousin. Had to leave it in back in Los Angeles."

A flash of red, the color of blood, produced Cole, Ares's favorite grandson. "Titus, I refuse to take up golfing, fishing, playing bridge, or any of the leisurely activities our elders do. What the fuck has happened?"

"Seriously, wait for the others," Jayson said. "We all deserve to hear this fuck up."

"I agree." Titus felt the weight of his failure on his shoulders. He'd failed his cousins who had helped him launch Love Ink.

The newest generation of Olympians had dreamed of a day their divinity could be released, allowed to flourish in the world, if only a little. For decades, he and his cousins had worked on the plan. The tattoo shop was to be the first step that would eventually allow all of them to work covertly in a few mortals' lives without the knowledge of Zeus and the other elders. They'd all made sacrifices for years, secretly hiding away a good share of their rations of ambrosia, which were now stored here in the shop. They'd all denied themselves much for a vision, a hope, and a new way of existing. Now that dream was gone for good.

Lukus, Poseidon's grandson materialized in a swirl of blue water, wearing a black leather jacket, a designer shirt, and Italian shoes. His dark hair and beard were perfectly trimmed. No matter how many times Titus saw Lukus teleport without getting a drop of the liquid on his clothes, it still amazed him. His aquatic cousin took a step forward, splashing the puddle left behind by his transport.

"Damn it, Luke. You're going to mop that up, not me," Kyros growled.

"Sure thing, buddy," the water demigod said.

Atreus and Zil, grandsons of Apollo materialized together in a flash of yellow light. They were mirror images of each other with their dark hair and buff, chocolate-colored bodies. Zil wore surfer shorts and nothing else, while Atreus wore torn jeans and boots.

"Do you two ever wear shirts?" Kyros asked. "This is a place of business you know."

Atreus smiled and placed his hand out in front of him, palm up. Out of thin air, he produced two T-shirts. "Here brother," he said, holding one of them out for Zil. "I guess we are a bit underdressed for this crowd."

Last to arrive was Krystal, granddaughter of Dionysus. Her long blonde curls fell past her shoulders. The dress she had on was blood red and revealed the cleavage of her ample breasts. She looked around the room. "I see the gay brigade is all here."

"For the last time, Krystal, I'm not gay," Zil said.

"No? The jury is still out on that one, I think." She winked. "My elder brother is so pissed, Titus, and I bet once my other two brothers find out, they will be too."

"Why?" he asked.

"For excluding them in our rebellion, of course. Let me see if I can get this right. And I quote, 'Just because I'm not gay doesn't mean I wouldn't have wanted to join them in this. They're a bunch of reverse bigoted assholes, if you ask me. If they want my help, tell them to call. I'm still on board if they haven't fucked things up too much.' End of quote."

"Fuck Evan," Daemon said. "We did talk to him about it a long time ago, but he told us we were crazy."

"He didn't believe we were serious, Daemon," Cole said.

"Too bad for him." The dark demigod sat down in one of the chairs.

"We all know why we gravitated to this core group, don't we?" Lukus asked. "We were gay. That was the commonality between us."

"That was the only thing," interjected Kyros.

"I'm not gay," Zil said again. "Neither is Krystal."

"None of this matters." Titus was ready to spill his guts and be done with it. "Who was in on this or not doesn't matter anymore. Zeus knows. Everyone knows. It's over."

Was it over for him and Derek, too? That thought crushed him even more than knowing all that he and his cousins had strived for was lost.

Krystal put her arms around him. "It's going to be okay. You'll see."

"Always the optimist," he said.

"Everyone, take a seat," she said to the others. "Let's hear Titus out. I bet we can salvage this. The elders know some but they don't know everything." She turned to Kyros. "Your dad is doing some fancy maneuvering with the council. All is not lost."

"You can't believe that, Krystal," Titus said.

"But I do. And so should you." She plopped down to the floor, crossing her legs. "Spill it. Every bit of it."

He looked around the room as his cousins began settling in for the debriefing. On all their faces he could see signs of hope popping up, all a result of Krystal's cheerleading and positive attitude.

Hope sprung up inside him, may the ancients find mercy. They'd all worked too hard to get here. He loved helping humankind. There were four men still alive and well and in love all because his divine spark had been inked onto their flesh. That had to be worth fighting for. Even more, he was in love for the first time in his life. He wasn't sure why Derek had bolted, but he was going to find out. He wasn't about to give up on having a life with him. Derek would be his. He would make sure of that if he had to crush heaven and earth to do it.

Cole jumped up. "Fuck. I've got to go."

"Now?" Kyros asked. "Surely whatever you have to do can wait until later."

"I'm being summoned."

"By who?" Daemon asked.

"By my grandfather."

Shit. Titus could always hope for a miracle. "Your father's dad?"

"No. My mother's."

Harmonia's father was Ares. *Him ordering Cole to his side can't be good.*

"Why would he be summoning you now?" Zil asked.

"Who knows?" Cole shook his head. "You know he only calls on me for the dirty jobs. Or he might just want to have dinner with me to talk about his old glory days. It could be either of those. I want all the deets about this, Titus. Got me?"

"You'll get them. I swear."

∼

DEREK SAT at his desk staring dully at his computer. It was eight a.m. Only four hours left to find a murderer. The vision from last night had been seared in his memory cells. *What the fuck do I do now?* If the image turned out to be true, then the obvious leap was to believe Titus was responsible for the three murders. But what if it wasn't true? What if his gift had finally misfired? He was grasping at straws, but straws were all he had.

"Stone, get in here," Lieutenant Gray's voice shook him from his thoughts.

He stood and walked into the commander's office, wondering what misstep of his had once again pissed the man off. "What can I do for you?"

Gray sat behind his desk with an open folder in front of him. "Always a smartass, hey, Stone?"

"Sir?"

"Take a seat, Detective."

He sat down.

Gray closed the file on his desk and looked him straight in the eyes. "I've talked to the assistant D.A. He's not ready to go for an arrest with what we have, but I think your intuition is on the money. You and your partner get to Love Ink. Question the bastard again. Find me something that will stick so we can get that warrant."

Derek couldn't bear the thought of Titus behind bars. In his heart, he believed him innocent, no matter what his mother's curse had shown him. Taking an oath to uphold the law was something he'd taken very seriously when he'd become a police officer. The vow had been the one constant in his life. No matter what, he'd always abided by it. But how could he do that now? Even though he didn't really believe in love, he definitely felt something for Titus, something strong and powerful. Call it caring, infatuation, lust—its name didn't matter, only saving the man who'd given him hope to live again did.

He put his hand up to his chest where the ink that Titus had given him resided underneath his shirt. Unlike the victims' tats he'd felt, this one was completely closed to him, to his gift. It seemed like an ordinary piece of skin art, but its power had worked back at Love Ink. He'd surrendered to its sway which led him to be intimate with Titus. Perhaps since it was on his flesh, the spell was masked, hidden from him and his mother's curse.

Please let the magic hold.

"Commander, I've already been to Love Ink twice to question Mr. Love. He's squeaky clean," he lied, thanking the heavens for the magic of Titus's tat.

"Are you getting cold feet on this one, Stone?"

"No. I think we need to talk to Barnes's nephew."

"Explain to me how the nephew of Samuel Barnes..." Gray looked down at the open folder in front of him. He turned a few pages, read something, and then looked back at him. "A Mr. Kyle Pippins has any connection to Paul Crane?"

His mind riffled through every memorized fact of the case in the hopes of drawing any line of logic to get the commander off of Titus's scent. Thankfully the power of the tattoo seemed to be stronger than the badge over him. "I'm not sure yet, but once I get to talk to—"

Gray held up his hand in the universal sign of "stop." "Don't bull-shit me, Stone. I want to hear what you have."

"I'm not sure what you want me to say." Again, he lied. Deceiving Gray didn't make any sense, especially given his earlier vision about Love. Getting Titus incarcerated might actually save his life. And yet here he was, doing just that.

His commander glared at him. "Let me give you a piece of advice, Stone."

"Yeah, sure."

As Gray stood and came around the desk, he got up to his feet, readying to meet him eye to eye. "It's not too late to turn things around for you, for your career here. Your talented, Derek. Really talented. You see things others miss. There's no limit to where you could be in another year or two. Maybe at this desk. There are people that want to help you, and I'm one of them. All I ask is that you be honest with me."

He had to give it to Gray. The man had shot up the ladder at rocket speed, and was obviously not satisfied with his current posi-tion. There were new heights for the DPD's brightest star to climb. "Are you offering me your job, Commander?"

"Cut the crap. You know what I mean. Whatever is holding you back on this case, get rid of it, squash it, and bury it." Gray's eyelids narrowed. "You see something in that magical head of yours, don't you?"

It was the first time Derek's boss had ever spoken of his curse. "What are you talking about, sir?"

"Fuck, Stone. I know. Everyone knows. Hell, my very first day on the job, Deputy Chief Moore talked to me about you and your...talents."

"I'm not following you," he said, though in truth he totally understood Gray's point.

"You're tough to rein in but your special skills are needed in this unit, especially now. So, are you going to tell me what your unusual intuition showed you about these murders? About Titus Love?"

He froze at the mention of his name. No way would he betray him. The murderous vision from before threatened to reappear and overwhelm him again. He shoved it down to the back of his mind with his will.

"Stone, you better not be holding anything back from me."

"I'm not. I'd love to tell you my crystal ball provided me with some evidence, but it's on the fritz."

"A joke? You've got to be kidding." Gray shook his head in apparent frustration. "Fine. Your way then for now. You will come around, Stone. I always get my way in the end. You'll see. I want to be in the loop on every part of this case, you understand me?"

"Yes, sir."

"Where's your partner?"

"I honestly don't know."

"Vende thinks he's special because his mother is in congress. That's doesn't mean a damn thing to me."

"I didn't know that about him."

Gray sighed. "Find him and both of you head back to Love Ink. Look for anything that will give you an excuse to bring our suspect in. Am I clear?"

"Yes, sir."

"He's guilty of something. I know it, and you know it, too. Now get the fuck out of my office."

9

Titus placed another bottle on the table in front of him. He closed his eyes and willed it away to the space Kyros had secured.

Still no word from Olympus, which might've meant Uncle Notos had fixed things there, or at least smoothed them over as he'd promised. *By Olympus' itself, let that be true.*

All his cousins were gone, each onto an agreed upon task. They'd split up to protect the five mortals he'd given tats to with the ink enchanted by his grandfather's arrow. Atreus and Zil were guarding one each. Krystal and Kyros went invisibly to the third. Jayson and Lukus watched over the fourth. Daemon, who always worked alone, circled the fifth.

Cole had not returned.

Titus set three more bottles of the godly nectar on the table. He waved his hand, and they vanished to the storage unit Kyros had secured.

Before leaving, Krystal had begged him to limit the teleportation of the ambrosia stock to no more than three at a time. "Please say you'll restrain yourself," she'd said. "Keep it to three bottles or three loaves. Or any combination of them, as long as your count remains a maximum of three. You must conserve your energy in case 'you know who' shows up."

By "you know who," did Krystal mean the Olympian elders, the Promethean bastards, or Derek? He wasn't certain.

Derek. He longed to see him again, to hold him in his arms. All his cousins thought the gorgeous detective was too dangerous, a risk to their family. He'd not asked Krystal to clarify her "you know who" but had agreed to limit himself. Still, he was concerned about how long this was taking. His power didn't seem to have gone down much at all during the process.

He looked at the cases and cases of ambrosia nectar and loaves still to be sent out of the shop. If Prometheans were close, the last thing he or his cousins wanted was to give them more ammo for their horrible deeds.

But it wasn't just the evil devotees Titus had to worry about suddenly appearing at the shop. If the elders showed up to inspect, they would expect to find the appropriate amounts of ambrosia on hand for two young demigods, not an army of immortals.

Calling forth the divine spark inside him, he willed all the crates of food to the storage unit. As the power left him, a bright light surrounded the ambrosia containers, and then all but a single bottle and half loaf he'd left in the back room disappeared.

"Sorry, Krystal," he said aloud, knowing no one was around to hear.

The sparse amount of divine food and drink remaining would've lasted him and Kyros a couple of months or more with normal consumption, but these dark times demanded they and their cousins become gluttonous and disobey the council's decrees.

If the three murders were the work of Prometheans, they would certainly try to kill another of Love Ink's customers. When the fuckers showed up, his cousins would be ready—as best they could—each having earlier downed an entire bottle of the nectar of the gods. His cousins were juiced up to the max.

If, on the other hand, some psychotic bastard had taken out the three humans and not their ancient enemies, Titus's cousins would easily dispose of that mortal. He prayed for the later to be the case, unsure how a battle with Prometheans would end even with the large amount of ambrosia flowing through his and his cousins' veins.

WILES LOOKED at the thick stakes of Benjamins on the coffee table and knew he didn't have enough. He'd kept the last bag of ice he'd conjured. He'd need it for his trip.

Selling the rest of the shit to pad his wallet had been easy for him. Like riding a bicycle, old talents never went away completely. The meth was pure and kicked like a motherfucker. After taking a freebie hit, every one of his customers had paid dearly for the crap. No wonder, since he'd created it out of thin air with the supernatural hocus-pocus he'd stolen from his last victim.

No more power was left inside him. *Fuck.*

He'd had to activate a big portion of the magic to keep Sam's goddamn nephew from kicking him out of the penthouse when he'd arrived late last night. He would've killed the son of a bitch had he not brought an attorney, moving men, and two deputy sheriffs with him. Too many assholes to deal with at one time, even for him.

He looked around the living room that had been filled with treasures less than a day ago. Sam's heir had removed everything of real value so there was nothing left to pawn. Too bad all the supernatural shit was gone. *Now what?* He'd counted the stacks, and while he had several thousand, he needed more. Hell, more money and more of the good stuff he'd drained off of Sam and Paul. He'd fucked up.

The doorbell rang. *Shit. If that's Sam's nephew, I'm going to slam his head into the wall.*

He scooped up the money and ice and put it all in the backpack he'd tossed on the chair.

Again, the doorbell rang. "Hold your fucking horses, asshole," he whispered. No sense in tipping off whoever was in the hallway that he was home.

He walked to the door, placing his right hand on the pistol he'd tucked into the back of the waist of his jeans. Then he looked through the peephole and saw a blonde woman in a dark suit on the other side of the door.

Was this bitch another ambulance chaser Sam's nephew had hired?

He opened the door. "Yes?"

"Hello, Mr. Underwood." The woman had the oddest colored eyes he'd ever seen—gray. He guessed her to be in her early thirties. There was something about her, something strange, though he couldn't put his finger on what exactly gave him pause. If he needed to pull out his forty-five, he would. In an odd way, he hoped he would need to do it. The three murders had brought him to life. He loved seeing the victims' cold empty eyes. He relished the absolute control he held over them. "And you are?" he asked the skank who just might be his victim number four.

"I'm Ms. Carver, Ms. Daphne Carver, and I have a proposition for you. May I come in?"

"The deal was for another week, so get the fuck out of here and tell that goddamn prick he'll get this apartment on Sunday and not a day before."

"Mr. Underwood, I apologize for the confusion. I'm not representing Mr. Barnes's nephew. I'm here on another matter entirely."

"What matter?"

"Let me in and the...shall we say...the invisible boost you received recently can be renewed." Ms. Carver held out her hand, palm up. An inch above the woman's fingertips appeared a ball of red light the size of a half dollar. "Let me prove to you I'm on your side, Mr. Underwood. Take it."

"How?" his heart thudded in his chest.

"You know how. Just take it."

He placed his hand over the floating ball of light. Like an ice cube, it melted, not down, but up into his hand, into his body, into his everything. The power of the magic burned his insides like lava, but it also felt amazing. "Where did you get that?"

"Not important, Mr. Underwood. I would think you would be more concerned about getting more of the same kind of power you got off the tats of your boss and the other man. There's so much more of it than you can imagine. You're one of the few mortals to have tasted such pure energy."

"How do I do that, exactly? It was happenstance that I stumbled onto this."

"Not happenstance. You're special. You have a gift. Have you ever noticed how you sometimes know what people are going to say before they say it? That's not just coincidence. You're descended from very special humans. Very special indeed."

In the back of his mind, a little pinprick of pain told him not to trust this woman with her blonde curls, heaving chest, and bright red lips, but the energy swirling inside him was only a taste of what was to come. If this bitch wasn't lying, he would soon have enough power to make all his dreams come true and have a chance to dream even bigger dreams.

DEREK SAT inside his vehicle trying to manage his will to go inside and face Titus, the man he'd been sent to grill to get either a confession or enough evidence to bring him down. He didn't have a single good reason to remain in the car. His task was clear.

His cell buzzed, indicating a text message had just arrived. He glanced down at the name of the sender, Michael Vende. Derek had sent his partner on a wild goose chase so that he could fly solo to Love Ink. Instead of reading the message, he hit the button that turned the screen off.

His rational side had clearly vacated the premises of his mind. Was Titus's tat on his chest impacting him? His mother's curse didn't help him know. In fact, the damn psychic shit was silent, which in the past would've made him extremely happy but now only made things worse for him—and maybe for Titus, too.

All he wanted to do now was bolt out of the car and into the tattoo shop, find Titus, throw him to the ground and make love to him. Ridiculous and foolish. Would it only be sex? Another trick? A random fuck? That had been Derek's M.O. for the past few years. Find a target, seduce them to bed, fuck them senseless, and then send them on their way before the sun came up. Easy. Fuck'em-and-forget'em Stone. Why was his dick arguing with him now? He was rock hard, and believing Titus was inside the tattoo shop—a mere fifty feet from him—had his pulse pounding hard and fast.

His calls to a few of Titus's past customers confirmed the handsome beast was single, but that didn't mean Love was looking for something more permanent, more forever.

Fuck. What the hell am I thinking? I'm acting like I'm in love with him. Not possible. First, they'd only known each other a very short time. Second, they were apparently on opposite sides of the law. Third, he didn't believe in the emotion of love. The whole concept of being with one man for the rest of one's life was ludicrous. He'd learned that long ago.

Images of Eros and Psyche floated in the back of his mind. He shook his head, willing them away. Black and white. That was how the world worked. He'd let his imagination get the better of him. No more. Not any longer.

He needed to remain focused. Gray's instructions had been very clear. Get something on Titus Love that would stick. Stepping out of the car, he took a deep breath. Tat or no tat, it was time to do what he did best—police work.

Walking into the shop, he found Titus alone. Like raw meat to sharks, his cock hardened even more.

"Hello." Love's multicolored eyes sparkled.

He met his gaze full on. "I have more questions for you, Mr. Love."

"I see. I must be in hot water since you're acting all über-cop. Cut the crap. Are you here to arrest me, Derek?"

Hearing Titus call him by name made his entire body stiffen, readying itself for sex. Was that why he was here? For sex and not for what Gray had sent him to do? He did feel like he was on a kind of autopilot. In reality, it didn't matter why. He was here. Titus was in trouble. Cop or not, just being in the same room with Love had his protective instinct switching on to full power. He had to find a way to remove suspicion from the man who had swept him off his feet, even if it ultimately meant relinquishing his badge.

"Titus, I want to help you. I know you're holding something back. Don't. It will only lead you down a path that ends with you behind bars. Trust me. I'm being lenient because I care."

"You do?" The corners of Titus's gorgeous mouth curved up. "You care about me?"

"Stop parroting me. My partner, Michael Vende, is back at the morgue talking to the medical examiner about her findings on the Barnes case," he confessed.

"Why are you telling me this, Derek? You're not acting like a homicide detective to me."

He didn't know why, but he believed in Titus, in his innocence. "Please, Titus. We don't have time for this. I care. Yes. It's true. But Vende won't remain in the dark for long. We have a very small window of opportunity to figure out a plan of action."

Titus stepped right in front of him. "Already on it, baby. I'll be fine. It's you I'm worried about."

"Me? I'm not the one who is the main suspect in three murders. You are."

"There's much more to this than you can imagine." Titus looked him in the eye. "Much more, my love. I'm so glad you're not a Promethean. I knew your heart had to be pure."

"What's a Promethean?" His mother's curse began to fire. Someone was coming. Vende? No, another person—or persons—filled with...what?

Power.

He pulled out his pistol and clicked off the safety.

"Get behind me and get low," Titus instructed in a whisper.

"What's going on?" he asked as the air sparked with electricity.

Before Titus could answer him, two people, a male and a female, materialized out of thin air. Kyros Swift appeared in the middle of the room with a woman in a red dress.

Derek's jaw dropped. *So much for things being black and white.*

Kyros looked directly at him. "Hello, Detective."

"That's him?" the woman asked, pointing his direction.

"Yes. That's Detective Stone," Swift answered. "Titus, you've got to get out of here, and if you care about your mortal, you better take him with you."

"Derek, this is Krystal. You know Kyros already." Titus turned back to the magical duo. "What's happened? Hell, I've only started working in the love business and have already gotten my hands bloody. Is there another mortal dead because of me?"

Derek's gut wrenched as his mother's curse blasted hot in his mind. "Another dead?" Had he been all wrong about Titus?

"No one is dead just yet," Krystal answered.

"Did the Prometheans show up?" Titus asked.

"No," Kyros answered. "The trouble we're in is that Ares isn't waiting for the twelve to convene. He's taking matters into his own hands and has instructed Cole to kill Detective Stone. That's why he summoned Cole in the first place."

"Did this Cole fellow kill Barnes?" Derek asked. "And can someone tell me what the hell the Prometheans are?"

Kyros shook his head. "Detective, you're in way over your head on this one, but no. Cole isn't the killer."

"Titus can fill you in on the rest later," Krystal said. "For now, you better get the fuck out of here. And fast."

Kyros closed his eyes, and Titus nodded.

"Got the location, cousin?" Kyros asked.

"Yes," Titus answered.

"Then go," Krystal said. "Go now. We'll do our best to keep you off of Cole's radar."

"Do better than that, Krystal. Please. I can't lose Derek. I won't."

Derek heard the threat in Titus's tone. Whoever this Cole person

—killer—might be, he'd bet that Titus would do his best to keep him safe, no matter what.

Titus wrapped him in his arms. "Brace yourself, sweetheart."

"For what?" And then it happened. The whole world melted away and his stomach lurched up into his throat. He felt like he was spinning wildly in a kind of void. And as fast as it had begun, it was over.

10

Titus held Derek close to him, sensing the tension growing inside his detective. An immortal's first teleportation was jarring even though they prepared for it with their parents for a few years. Derek was mortal with no clue about instantly moving from one place to another on a beam of light.

"What the hell did you do to me?" his mortal asked, his legs seeming to give way, but Titus held him up.

"I'm so sorry about all of this."

The air was chilled enough to make their breaths visible. He looked around to get his bearings, since he'd never seen or even known about Uncle Notos's secret cabin.

"Where the hell are we? How did you do this?" Derek held his gun in his shaking hand, which apparently comforted him just a bit, though his eyes darted frantically around the room with the knotty pine wood walls.

"Put the gun down, Derek. We're safe."

"Safe? From who? Cole? Who is he? What about you? Where are we?" A million other questions and concerns must've been racing through Derek's mind.

"Relax, sweetheart," he said. "We're safe in my uncle's cabin."

"Where exactly are we? What city?" Derek kept the gun aimed at him. He couldn't blame him, not one bit.

"Antarctica, about two hundred miles from the South Pole on the thirty-second latitude. This is my Uncle Notos's secret hideaway. No one should find us here."

Cabin wasn't quite the right word to describe this place. It looked extremely high end, typical for Kyros's dad. He liked his creature comforts. Two stone fireplaces were on opposite walls of one another and seemed to be the only heat sources in the space, though he knew better. The air vibrated with residual magic. The scent of seasoned oak filled his nostrils, warming his insides, making his visible breath invisible once again. Titus willed some of his inner power to warm the space to a more comfortable temperature.

The furniture looked very expensive, though comfortable. A flat screen television behemoth was attached to another wall at the perfect height for viewing. On the table just below the TV was every kind of movie you could imagine in DVD. A large mahogany bookshelf sat to the side loaded with sculptures and a couple of dozen board games. On the window's sill sat not one, but two sets of binoculars, obviously meant for wildlife watching. On the other side of the window's glass, on what looked to be an expansive wooden porch was a telescope pointing up at the star-filled night sky.

"This doesn't look like a common cabin. This looks more like a mansion, Titus."

"My family has money. What can I say?"

"How aren't we freezing to death? Those..." his sweet mortal said, pointing to the large windows looking out to the frozen tundra. "Shouldn't they be thick portholes to hold back the killing cold, not thin panes of glass?"

"How do I say this?" He wasn't sure where to begin. Derek knew more than humans were allowed, but things had moved long past keeping up appearances, that was for sure. Ares had ordered a hit.

"Tell me, Titus. I already had some ideas about you after all my research into the Barnes's murder case. After this unbelievable trip to Antarctica, I'm pretty sure my suspicions were right all along."

"You deserve the truth. All of it. This whole place is spelled, filled with Notos's magic. Being the god of the Southern winds, his power here is quite high."

"Got it. God of the Southern winds." Derek took a deep breath and then let it out slowly. "Your cousins, Eros and Psyche...they are the actual god of love and goddess of the soul?"

"Not exactly." He studied more of the cabin's trappings. They were safe here. They could take some time to get to know each other better, which was exactly how he wanted it. If things heated up and Cole got too close, which was unlikely given Uncle Notos's skill at hiding things, Kyros and Krystal would come first and warn him so he could whisk Derek away to another place of safety. "You're right and you're wrong about Eros and Psyche."

"What do you mean?" Derek holstered his gun.

"Yes, they *are* the god of love and goddess of the soul, but they *are not* my cousins. They are my grandparents and they are immortal."

Derek nodded, fixing his chocolate eyes on him. "Are you immortal, too? A god of some sort?"

A jolt shot up and down his spine, thinking about that little tidbit. "I'm immortal, sweetheart, but I'm not actually a god."

"Demigod then," Derek corrected.

"In title only, not in function. Not really either now. Not anymore." The elders would most definitely strip him of his title after all of this. Even if by some thin chance they didn't, he still would not risk another human life for his petty need to impact mankind. "Are you hungry?"

Derek frowned. "Don't try to get me off topic, Mr. Love."

"Stop calling me that, please." But in truth, this man could call him anything and he would be okay with it, just as long as he got to be with him. "I'll answer all your questions, but that doesn't mean we shouldn't have a bite to eat while we talk."

"Shouldn't we stay alert in case this Cole fellow shows up unannounced?" Derek asked, pulling his gun back out from its holster and expertly taking stock of his weapon.

"He won't. We'll get word long before, if he can even find us, which I doubt."

"A magic cabin with priceless treasures in Antarctica, the Greek gods exist, and that you're one of them is a lot to digest." Derek put his pistol back in the holster once again. "How did your uncle get his money?"

"My whole family is loaded, not difficult to achieve when you have time on your side. Having money is important to them, and has been especially since retiring." He couldn't stop staring at the male beauty. Whatever it took, he would protect Derek from Cole, Ares, and if it came to it, Zeus himself. Derek was his, and he was Derek's now and forever. He would move heaven and earth until his sweet detective knew it, too.

"They're retired? All of them?"

"Have you ever been diagnosed with having attention deficit disorder, Detective?"

He frowned. "No. Why?"

Heat rushed to his cock and his heart fluttered in his chest. "You have a lot of questions, and none of them have to do with sex."

"I'm a detective. It's part of the job. Besides, who said we're going to have sex?"

"So you're not interested?" he asked, hoping to get under Derek's skin just a bit.

"The truth is, Titus, I haven't stopped thinking about how much I want to be next to you, naked, both of us, since we enjoyed each other in your office."

"Me either, Derek. Once isn't enough for me." He wanted a repeat, *threepeat, fourpeat*, and more. "Is it for you?"

"No. It isn't." His mortal smiled, which ignited an explosive need inside him. "But I think we need to remain focused on things. I'm way out of my element here. I have a lot more questions for you."

"Mark my words, Derek. We are going to have sex again." He smiled, feeling his lust for this man, *his man*, twist and burn inside his body. "I'll give you all the long answers you need *after* we make love. For now, the short ones will have to suffice you."

"That works for me." Derek's self-confidence was intoxicating and alluring.

Titus tamped down his desire. "Ask, Detective."

"Tell me about Barnes and Crane. What happened to them? Who killed them?"

"Their deaths were likely the work of Prometheans. They're the reason my family closed up shop. How do I explain this to you?" He closed his eyes, feeling the gravity of the past four thousand years pressing on him like the mythic rock that held the chained, captive god.

"At the start of all this, Titus. That's where you should begin."

He opened his eyes and gazed into Derek's chocolate orbs. Gods, the man was beautiful. More than that, he was strong and coura-geous. He was the one for him, the only one. "Ambrosia is the food of my family, but nothing compares to what adoration does for a god. Before retiring, Zeus and the others were much more than they are now. Worshipers' adoration juiced them up to the max, giving them power to bend the very fabric of reality in any way they saw fit. The more adoration they received, the more they wanted. It became their drug of choice. Used sparingly, adoration can be a tool to aid humans. Abused, it can become a weapon in the wrong hands. Prometheus loved his worshipers more than any other of my family."

"I remember the story of Prometheus. He brought fire and light to humankind, breaking the Olympian law. Zeus punished him by chaining him to a rock. Every day, vultures ate his organs, and every morning they grew back. Talk about hell. That would be hell."

He shook his head, hating the lies that still swirled in the world about the fallen god. "It was hell, but the myth was twisted by his followers, the Prometheans."

"Seriously?" Derek's eyebrows shot up.

"They were the original spin doctors. Prometheus shared his power with some of his priests as a reward for their devotion. How did they repay him? They turned on Prometheus, using his own power against him, making their own god their prisoner. Zeus, our kind, and some others tried to find him, but couldn't. Some of the other priests of the other gods, including a few of Zeus's, sided with the Prometheans. Zeus would've been captured had it not been for Uncle Notos, but that's another story for another time."

"These Prometheans are still around?"

"Yes, Detective." No mortal had ever heard the whole truth about Prometheus, other than the ones in the evil Order before Derek. "They are men and women of power, leaders in every facet of mortal existence you can imagine. Politicians. CEOs. Bankers. And more. All Olympians tread carefully in the world, unfortunately one or two lesser immortals are captured about every so often no matter how much we try to protect them. The last one—a river nymph named Chelsea—happened in France ten years ago."

"This is so surreal, Titus. I heard some of these stories in school. Most recently, I read up on them during my investigation. Hearing that they were real, historical even, is something I wouldn't have ever imagined."

"That's how the elders like things in the world of humans. They've worked very hard to keep mortals in the dark about their existence."

"And what about Prometheus? Was he ever found?"

Titus shook his head. "Some believe he is still alive at some secret Promethean hideout where the fuckers continue to drain his divinity. If so, he won't last much longer. Even immortals can be killed, though that seems like an oxymoron, doesn't it, sweetheart?"

DEREK LOOKED AT TITUS, the immortal, the demigod, the accused—the one he couldn't shake from his thoughts, his imagination, and his needs. "You may not like what I have to say about that, but I'm glad the gods aren't all-powerful, fearing nothing. If they can die, you can die, it makes you and your family seem more human to me. I like knowing that." He felt his stomach roll and realized it had been a while since his last meal. "You offered food a moment ago. Is that still on the table?"

"Yes it is. I'm famished. Let's see what we can find."

"You immortals have to eat like we do? Humans, I mean." A million other questions rolled through his mind that he wanted to ask this gorgeous creature. *Gorgeous creature? What have I gotten myself into?*

"I can starve, if that's what you're asking me, Derek, but it would take several centuries or millennia for me to die. Like you, I need food for energy."

As if they'd just arrived at a little getaway for some much deserved R&R, he followed Titus to the kitchen. Its style was country, offering every amenity of appliance, including a cappuccino machine. Inside the bottom drawer freezer of the French-style refrigerator, they found only frozen TV dinners, nothing more. In the main compartment of the appliance was three bottles of deep red liquid. Wine? God, he could sure use some right now.

"Shall I get us some glasses for wine?" he asked. *When in Rome, or Antarctica, as we are now...*

"This isn't wine, Derek. This is ambrosia."

"Ambrosia? You mentioned it earlier. You said it was the food of your family. I read that it is the food of the gods."

"Yes, and you should have a glass of it just in case."

"In case this Cole guy shows up? How will that help me?"

Titus cupped his chin. "It'll give your powers a boost and might just save your life, sweetheart. Not too much, though. It can give quite a kick between the eyes the next day for most mortals. But you're not like most mortals, are you?"

He shrugged. "A divine hangover?"

Titus nodded. "You look like a steak and potato man to me. Am I right?"

"I am, but I see only this ambrosia stuff and the TV dinners."

"Leave it to me, Derek. How do you like your steak cooked?"

"Medium rare." He wasn't sure where Titus was going to find a steak in the middle of this frozen wasteland, but it sounded delicious right now.

"Good deal."

"How old are you, Titus?"

"You really want to know?" The sexy demigod tilted his head to one side slightly. "I don't want to say if it will change things between us, Derek."

"Change things? What things?" he asked, but already knew the answer. Apparently Titus's emotions for him were growing as fast as his were for the immortal. "Slow down cowboy. We really just met yesterday."

"Love doesn't obey timelines, Detective. Most times it takes a year or more for it to really bloom, but sometimes it explodes in the hearts of two lovers with such intensity they cannot resist but collide into each other's arms. I think that is what is happening with you and me, Detective. Don't you?"

Titus's words melted his hesitation, his logic, and the walls he'd built around his heart. And yet the old memories fueled his doubts, remained, though lessened by the proximity, the closeness of this amazing immortal. "Slow down, mister. You've got some very impressive lines. They work on all the boys? I only wanted to know how old you are. If it's too much to ask, I take it back."

"My birthday is March twenty-ninth, if you're thinking about buying me a present." Titus's multicolored eyes fixed on him, devastating every inch, every fiber of his being. When the demigod released his gaze, turning to the kitchen counter, Derek felt a maddening hunger, not from his gut but lower, expand and multiply inside him.

"What can I do to help with this meal?"

"See if there are some glasses for our drinks."

He walked over to the sink. "You still avoided answering my question fully, mister. I'm not letting you off the hook that easy." Crazy as it might seem, he really did want to know Titus's age. "What year were you born?"

The wall cabinet to the left had crystal wine glasses. He grabbed two.

"I was born in seventeen eighty-three in Philadelphia," the divine being who wrecked him through and through, stated categorically.

Fuck. He's well over two hundred years old. Taking a deep breath to calm his nerves, Derek turned around, spotting two plates with sizzling New York strips and steaming baked potatoes next to Titus. *Amazing—the magical meal and the sexy god.* "With your skills, you could definitely push the microwave manufacturers in the world into bankruptcy. What else can you do?"

"Many things, but this is one of my best talents, Detective." Titus pressed his full lips against Derek's mouth, causing more than the temperature in the room to heat up.

When their kiss ended, Derek was soft around every one of his edges—fuzzy.

"Dinner is served," Titus said, placing the plates of food on the table.

He grabbed a bottle of the godly liquid and filled the two glasses he'd found.

They finished their magical meal and a couple of glasses of the sweet ambrosia in a hurry. His mother's gift reacted well to the liquid, causing him to buzz from head to toe. He looked at Titus and saw him, really saw him. A golden glow surrounded his amazing form. "You're beautiful, Mr. Love."

"And so are you, Detective Stone. So are you."

Now sipping on their third glasses, he gazed into Titus's eyes. "What are you?"

"I already told you, sweetheart. I'm an immortal."

"I know that, but who are you? I don't care about the myths, Titus. I want to get to know you. The real you."

"Actually, I'm an immortal who fucked up and broke Olympian law and now three mortals are dead." Titus's tone seemed filled with stinging regret.

"What law?"

"I told you about how the elders want to keep the human world in the dark. They achieve this by denying any divine intervention or assistance to any mortal. The paths between gods and humans were severed long ago. I opened up Love Ink, giving in to my nature. Derek, everyone in my family is drawn to help humanity. It's in our very blood, our very essence. So, I gifted a few humans enchanted tats so that they could find love." His immortal's face clouded with apparent guilt.

"That's a noble thing to do, Titus. A very noble thing."

"I should've never been so foolish to think the Prometheans wouldn't notice. Because of me, now you're in danger."

"Why did you pick me, Titus? I know I asked you to, but I'm not sure why you did."

The demigod's eyebrows shot up. "Pick you? I don't understand."

"You gave me one of your magical tats. I read up on the symbol and found it came from one of your granddad's temples a long time ago. It must have powerful mojo. It sure has worked a number on me. Believe me when I say I'm glad you did, I wouldn't change a thing about what has happened to me. But I really want to know why."

Titus laughed. "You think your tat is magical? That it's the reason you have worked to help me out of this mess?"

"Yes. What's so funny?"

His immortal leaned forward and kissed him, devouring his mouth once again. "Your tat has no magic. Yes, it is my grandfather's symbol, but I didn't make it with enchanted ink, Derek. What you've done, you've done on your own."

"That can't be true," he said, touching the place on his shirt where Titus's tat resided underneath the fabric.

The divine creature shrugged, placing his half-empty glass on the table. "It is true. Maybe you've done all of this out of love."

"I don't believe in love. It's nothing more than chemicals getting fired inside a person to make them act foolishly and believe more in someone than they should." Love got you hurt.

"I know you don't believe in love, but don't you wish you could? I bet you want to."

Derek sighed. "It doesn't matter if I do or don't want to. It doesn't really exist. Not for me at least."

Titus frowned, his sexy full mouth turning down. "Sweetheart, how can you say that after all you've seen? Miracles exist. They have for a very long time. Love is hard. That's true. But like miracles, love does happen for those who take the risk."

"Titus, I want you, magic ink or not. That's true. But it's only about sex. That's all it can be about for me." The old wounds of betrayal ached with fresh stings. *I have to protect my heart.* "I'm sorry if that hurts you. I think you're amazing. What gay man wouldn't? You're a demigod, and a very hot one to boot. But I'm not a commit-ment kind of guy. I can never be what you want." What he'd suffered from the breakup from Bill would look infinitesimal if he dared to venture the street of "happily ever after" with Titus only to find a split down the road. No way could he risk that kind of pain, that kind of torture.

"You don't have all the facts, Derek. You're everything I've ever dreamed of. You're perfect in every way. I've never loved anyone like I do you."

Titus was wrong about him. What did he have to offer an immor-tal, especially one as incredible as him? Nothing. Sex was okay with Derek. Love just wasn't in the cards. He needed to focus on some-thing else. "You really think Cole won't find us here?"

"Don't try to change the subject. That's my expertise, not yours. No. He shouldn't find us. My other cousins are on the job right now leading him down dead ends."

"How long can they keep that up?"

"For as long as it takes. Krystal or Kyros should show up and give us an update. Everything is going to be okay." But Titus didn't sound convincing, and his face clouded. "While we wait, tell me about the guy who hurt you so much that now you don't believe in love—or in me."

"No fair. I believe in you, but our age difference is a bit daunting. Talk about robbing the cradle. I'm thirty-one. You're just shy of a couple hundred years older than me. Wow." Laughing, he reached over and traced his finger over Titus's square jawline. "Still, I've always been attracted to older men."

"I want to talk about this," Titus said, leaning back just out of reach of Derek's touch.

"Chatting isn't really my thing. But sex is," he said, hoping to get things on track for some hot—über-hot—lovemaking.

"Stop sidestepping this. I want to hear about your ex, Derek. Now."

"Simple. Bill and I were together for a couple of years. I came home early one day to surprise him with a birthday present. I found him in our bed with two other guys fucking. Daytime soap opera material, if you must know." The acid in the back of his throat intensified as he continued telling the old tale. "After I kicked his ass out of my place, the truth surfaced quickly. He'd been cheating on me from the very first week we'd moved in together. I'm a detective, and I missed all the signs."

Titus leaned forward across the table, pushing their plates to the side. "Did you love Bill?"

"I thought I did, but no. I cared for him, but I really never loved him. Maybe that's why he cheated on me. He must've known in some way."

"Derek, don't blame yourself for your ex's fuck ups. Those are his alone."

"Sure. Whatever." If his cock was going to get any action, this discussion needed to end and soon. "How about we get naked, Demigod? I've been ready for hardcore fucking with you since our oral fun in your office."

"How romantic of you, Detective." Titus downed the last of his drink, the god juice. "I need to run some checks just in case Cole finds a way to us."

"Now you seem to be avoiding things," he said.

The immortal who kept chipping away at his invisible armor, reaching deeper into him than anyone had ever done, stood. "I'm not going to be with you, Derek, if you don't love me. Got it?"

Derek knew by his tone he meant it. He'd been in a daze ever since meeting Titus, but an admission of love wasn't possible. Sure, he was everything he wanted in a man. Protective to a fault. Titus had brought him to the bottom of the globe to keep a divine assassin sent by the god of war from killing him. No doubt there were bigger consequences to this action for the demigod than he was telling.

He could still feel Titus's mouth swallowing his cock, draining him of every drop of his seed. His rough beard on his legs had felt amazing. And Derek had tasted the demigod's dick, too. It was thick and long, like a beast with its own mind and will, a beast he would surrender to willingly. He wanted to have Titus inside his body.

Titus shook his head and then turned away. Derek stared at his back, trying to determine how the hell he was going to make him understand. It wasn't Titus he was resisting. It was love. Bill's betrayal had crushed him, and now he knew that he'd never really loved him, not like this sexy immortal. What would happen if Titus ended things? It wasn't that he thought the tat artist would cheat on him, but what did he really know about him? They'd only spent a few moments together. No days. No weeks. Just a few hours. Ridiculous. But those hours had been the best of his life. Still, what could a man who had lived over two hundred years want with him? Titus could have anyone.

"I'll clear the dishes," he said, hoping a mundane task might clear his head.

"Thanks, Detective." A line of white light shot from Titus's fingertips to the walls of the cabin.

"What's that?" he asked in awe.

"Insurance I should've already put in place, but I've been a bit distracted by you since we got here. It won't keep anyone out, but if any immortal crosses the line I'll feel it instantly."

The immortal was quite distracting to him, too. He stood and gathered up the dishes. "All this magic is overwhelming. I thought the psychic stuff I'd gotten from my mother was strange. Here, I feel like I've jumped into the looking glass and can't get out."

"You'll be free of me soon enough," Titus stated flatly.

He'd seriously screwed things up with him. Why did he always push people away whenever they got too close? Liz was the only one who kept coming back for more abuse. Everyone else had given up a long time ago. "I'm sorry, Titus."

"For what, Derek? For what exactly?" The edge in his tone was painfully sharp. "Talk to me. Tell me what you're feeling. Don't I deserve at least that?"

"Of course you do." He hated seeing the pain and anger in Titus's face. "It's not you. It's me."

The demigod faced him with his hands folded across his chest. "Go on."

"The truth? I chose Bill as a partner because he was safe. I didn't know it at the time, but that was why. I did care for him even if I didn't love him."

"Why settle for something less?"

This was hard to explain. "Because I've seen the thin line love and hate walk together. Do you know how many murders are committed by people who thought they were in love?"

"So you still think I'm the killer? Barnes and Crane and the coffee jockey are my doing?"

"No, I don't. You're no killer, but you could thrash my heart. You want the truth?" Every past loss welled up inside him, threatening to shut off the flood of words, but he tamped the memories down just enough to continue to open up to his immortal. "I'm terrified of you. Yes, I've fallen for you. Heaven help me. But is that enough?" His heart ached, but he tried to harden his resolve. Titus's world was not his, would never be his. He didn't have a footing there. His mother's curse had forced him to face the invisible from time to time. With Titus, he would have to live and breathe in that world every single second of every single day for the rest of his life, if and only if they could make it work. He just couldn't be sure. "Things end, Titus. Maybe not for you and your kind, but for mortals they end. Always. I won't survive if I give in to love, of that I'm sure."

Titus walked around the table and wrapped his arms around him. "That *is* the truth about your feelings, my love. You're scared. So am I. This is new for both of us. But I can assure you absolutely, unequivocally, without a doubt that you and I are in love."

Leaving before his heart was crushed was necessary, but this was Antarctica. There was no place to go, no place to hide. Looking at

Titus, he could imagine surrendering everything to the gorgeous man.

Titus squeezed him tighter. Had he sensed his hesitation?

He tensed. "Can you read my mind, demigod?"

"I should be asking you that, Derek." His multicolored eyes were kind and loving. "You're the one who has oracle powers, not me."

"What are you talking about?" he asked.

Titus kissed him again, melting his will to resist for good. "You love me, Derek." Another kiss. "You love me." Mouth to mouth again. "I know you love me." Titus's tongue entered his mouth, making him dizzy and hot. "Admission is all I ask. Once done, I will gladly make love to you, sweetheart. That's all it will take."

He wondered if he would ever be able to leave the gentle beast even after this assassin was taken care of. As their lips melded softly into one another's, a deep yearning for more shot up inside him, and his cock stiffened.

"You're a descendent of one of the great oracles, Derek. I'm sure you have powers you've dealt with your whole life. Right?"

"My mother called it a gift." He smiled a little, the memories of sitting next to her as she retold the stories of their family's unique talents rolling through his mind. "I always thought of it as a curse."

"Curse? It's no curse, my love. Listen to me carefully. There's likely been more times than not that your oracle powers have pulled you out of some tough spots. You need to trust in yourself and your gift."

"Easier said than done, I'm afraid."

"Yes. You're afraid. Afraid of your talents. Afraid of being hurt. Afraid of me. Afraid of love." Titus's multicolored eyes looked impossibly kind and genuine. "When will you stop being afraid? Aren't you tired of living this way, Derek?"

He was so very tired. Tired of being alone, so alone. "I am. You've opened my eyes in such a short time. Hell, we were just in Dallas an hour ago and here we are literally in the middle of nowhere." Derek reached up and touched his immortal's cheek, relishing the rough feel of his closely trimmed beard. "I care for you, Titus. I do. Very much. More than I've ever cared for anyone else. Can't that be enough for now?"

The sexy demigod smiled broadly. "Yes, my love. It's a great first step."

"Good. Now, take off your shirt," he demanded, craving the feel of Titus's skin against his.

"Somewhere in the playbook I'm sure there's a rule about oracles not commanding their deities," Titus said with a grin.

"Strip now." He pressed his lips to the man's throat and inhaled his hot scent.

"Works for me, sweetheart. And your clothes, too." Titus waved his hand and both their clothes vanished.

Derek stared into those multicolored eyes of his and felt deliciously warm. He moved his hands over Titus's powerful muscled chest. "I'm never going to get used to this supernatural stuff."

"You already have, Detective. Tell me about your gift." Titus sent his hand down to Derek's cock, wrapping meaty fingers around his shaft.

"First, I'd like my pistol back." Derek's heart pounded lustily in his chest.

"Still don't trust me, do you? Okay." Titus tilted his head slightly and Derek's gun and holster—only them and nothing more–were strapped once again to his side.

His Beretta might have no impact on Cole, but should the assassin cross Titus's line, he didn't want to be unarmed. "Thank you. About my gift. Mostly I sense things. Sometimes I have visions, but those come infrequently." He recalled the image of Titus kneeling over his corpse and felt a chill shoot up and down his spine.

"What's wrong, sweetheart? Your aura shifted suddenly."

Derek shoved the memory aside and moved his hands down from Titus's amazing chest to his ripped abs. Time had been good to his lover's physique. Very good. "Aura? You see mine?"

"I do, love." Titus smiled, nearly illuminating the room. "It's better now, but for an instant it darkened."

"Meaning?"

"A black aura can mean many things, but the most common is hopelessness. Yours has changed much since we first met. It's vibrating between orange, a sign of power, and red, a sign of sexual thoughts. There it goes, red again. You want me to suck your hard cock, Detective?" Titus asked with a wicked wink. "I'm happy to pleasure you, love, in any form you want."

"You're more beast than demigod, I bet." He kissed the man who had flipped his sense of things on its head. Reality wasn't as he'd imagined. Gods and goddesses existed. Who knew what else? And love? He was beginning to think it might actually exist too, as Titus believed.

"I'd enjoy showing you how much of a monster I can be, sweetheart." His lover pinched his nipples, delivering a nice passionate sting. "You like?"

"Uh-huh," was all he could mutter, staring into his eyes with the shiny flecks of silver and gold. Titus was definitely a mythical creature, massive and powerful. The demigod's confession of love for him had come so easy from his thick, gorgeous lips. Why was it so hard for Derek to do the same? He wasn't sure. In his entire life, he'd never felt more desired or wanted by another person. Those three words were right there vibrating on his lips, and still he remained silent. *Am I too fucked up to be with such a divine man as Titus?* The answer was a clear resounding "yes." "I want to tell you what you'd like to hear, Titus. I would. Hell, I should. You deserve that much from me."

His demigod took his face between his hands. "Sweetheart, you being with me now is reward enough. All I ask is for you to just feel and let go." Then Titus molded his mouth to his. As passion took Derek over completely, he wrapped one arm around Titus's shoulder and the other came around his waist. His lover did the same to him, a sensual symbol of equality between them.

"You have condoms stored here in Antarctica?" he asked teasingly.

"No need. Mortal diseases do not impact my kind. Anyway, your aura tells me you are in perfect health, Detective, and my eyes tell me everything about you is perfect." Titus's fingers trailed down his body, giving him a raging erection.

"So are you, demigod. So are you." He moved his hands all over the gorgeous beast's body, enjoying the brick-like frame of his torso. Reaching around behind him, he cupped Titus's ass and pulled him in tighter. "One day, I'll say those words to you. I'm sure of it. Just give me time."

"I'm immortal. I've got loads of time, love. I long for the day you are free to tell me what you feel." Titus sucked on his earlobe and slid his strong hands along his sides and down to his waist.

He closed his eyes, relishing the moment with this incredible man. He'd been so lost for so long until Titus came into his life. He tilted his head up as his demigod bathed his neck, causing heat to pump through his veins.

Less than what felt like a blink ago he would've never even imagined gods existed in the world, much less that he would be in the arms of one of them—an immortal tattoo artist. Never in his life did anything feel so right as touching and being touched by Titus. The invisible walls Derek had built around his heart were crumbling with every kiss, lick, and caress of his lover.

As Titus's hands feathered across his chest, lingering on his nipples, images began flooding into his mind. Visions. One was of Commander Gray standing by Derek's desk and shaking his head while talking to someone on his cell. Another was of Liz knocking on his door with a worried look on her face. No chance his iPhone had service here to call his boss and his friend to tell them he was safe. But was that fair to them when he didn't know for sure? Maybe not. Now, he only wanted to feel, to experience, to please and to be pleased. Titus was his world now. He didn't care if he ever went back to his old life.

11

"Where's my sweet oracle's mind off to now?" Titus gazed at the mortal who had given him more to live for than anything or anyone had done ever.

"Just thinking about you, Titus. Just you." Derek's tone was like the sweetest honey, his eyes like sparkling gems.

"I want to be inside you, Derek," he confessed. "And later I want you inside me. I want to feel closer to you than I have with anyone." He prayed for more time with his mortal, for a miracle that would end this nightmare seeking to destroy them, but his faith was thin.

"I want that, too." This man, this sweet detective, meant everything to him.

He lifted him up in his arms, and held him tight against his own body. He and Derek were similar in frame. His lover was strong and powerful, a man to have the respect of good friends and the fear of dangerous enemies. Their enemies were dangerous and immortal. The playing field advantage sat clearly with their opponents. One human and one young demigod weren't enough to stand against Olympus's wrath.

He'd told Derek, things would be okay, and for a brief moment, he'd believed the lie himself. But things for them would never be okay. Not with all that was against them. They could run and hide for a time, and maybe they would avoid detection for a month or two, but no more.

"Where's my immortal's head?" Derek asked smiling. "I think we might both suffer from ADD.

"I'm thinking about you, about us." Whatever time they had left together, he would make the most of it. Besides tasting every part of Derek's amazing body, what he craved more was to hear three specific words from his lover's mouth. "If I know my uncle, he's got a bedroom with all the comforts of home here." He carried Derek down the hallway and kicked open one of the doors. He looked at the gorgeous bathroom with the large garden tub big enough for both of them. "Wrong room, though we might have to take advantage of it later, my love."

"Your uncle has amazing taste. This looks more like a spa than a bathroom in a cabin."

"Immortals tend to like beautiful things, love." He kissed Derek again. "I'm just like them. I love beautiful things. And you, detective, are more beautiful than anything or anyone I've ever seen. Now, let's find that bed."

He needed Derek's walls to come down, all of them. If they were going to die, he wanted to do it in the arms of this man. Intoxicated by Derek's manly scent, he leaned into his neck and inhaled more of the sweet mortal's aroma into his lungs. He wanted to be inside Derek, feel the squeeze of his mortal's body on his dick.

"Here we go. Now this is more like it." He carried his sweet detective into the palatial bedroom, lowering him down on the silky sheets.

"Your family surely is loaded," Derek said, unbuckling his gun's holster. "I bet that's not too hard to do when you have centuries and centuries to learn the ins and outs of business and markets."

"Absolutely right, sweetheart. There's a shared mega international trust for all of us to draw from, but most immortals have their own money, too." He would love to shower Derek in all the world's best luxuries.

His darling detective placed his gun and holster under one of the pillows. "Forgive me for being crass, but what's your personal net worth?"

"Why? You want me to be your sugar daddy, love? That's a job I wouldn't mind at all."

He laughed. "I don't think I would fit into being a kept man, Titus. I'm just curious. According to my research, your Dallas home is valued at two million alone."

"You really did investigate me, didn't you?"

Derek's big eyes transfixed him. "That's my job. Or was my job, until today."

That last part crushed Titus. He wanted to tell Derek everything was going to be okay, that solving murders would once again fill his days, and Derek's nights would belong to him from now on. But lying to this mortal was no longer possible. "Last I checked I've got about ten million in real estate equity, stocks, bonds, and cash. That's actually pretty low for my family. Kyros's fortune is probably twice that."

He crawled on top of his sweet detective, pinning him to the mattress with only his frame. Body to body. Flesh to flesh. His mortal's erect cock slid next to his own dick, which was also rock hard.

"Do you like when I do this?" he asked, pinching Derek's nipples.

His lover's eyes glazed over and his eyelids fluttered. "Oh yes. I love it."

He kissed Derek again, sweeping his tongue past his lover's lips, creating a dance between his and Derek's tongues. Shifting his hip, grinding into the sweet detective, their cocks danced together, too, trapped between their midsections.

"What do you want, my love?" he asked Derek.

"I'm normally a top in the bedroom, but tonight I want to surrender to you."

His heart leapt for joy in his chest. Never had he been in such absolute sync and harmony with another in his entire life. "I want that, too, baby."

Derek's fingers threaded through his hair, raising the already blistering heat inside him several more degrees. "First, I want to taste you again, Titus, and then I want you inside me."

"Sounds good to me, but I think we should taste each other together. Sixty-nine can be fun, don't you think?"

"Actually, I've never done that before. I know it sounds strange. That should be a gay man's staple, but it's never been for me. I guess it felt too intimate up until now. But I would like to sixty-nine with you."

Titus could almost imagine this man, this wonderful amazing man, opening his mouth and uttering those three eternal words, a tender confession of true love. "You're too much my darling mortal." He shifted around on the bed. "Even the first gods would be amazed by you."

"Like I said before, you sure do have some of the best lines I've ever heard." Derek's hot breath skated over Titus's cock.

He wrapped his fingers around Derek's shaft, squeezing tenderly, enjoying the feel of him in his hand. When his mortal did the same to him, Titus closed his eyes, surrendering to the sensations zipping through his body. He wanted more than anything to give Derek pleasure, so he licked the tip of his cock, tasting the salty slickness, which was only a precursor of what was to come.

FEELING his lover's tongue on his cock's head sent Derek's years of pain and fear out the door and far away. He was Titus's, and Titus was his. Now and for the rest of his life.

Without hesitation and continuing to stroke his lover's shaft, he opened his mouth wide, granting the first intrusion of Titus's cock into him. When his immortal followed suit, devouring Derek's cock, every part of him began to vibrate. This wasn't another one-night-stand encounter. This was something much more. Being with Titus locked in a sixty-nine embrace had his heart wrapped up and flying with a million emotions. He wanted to be here, to experience his immortal's gifts fully. There wasn't another place in the world he'd rather be than here in this bed with Titus.

When his lover's finger began circling the tight ring of his ass, a jolt shot through him from where Titus touched him through his core and into his cock, which pulsed violently.

He sucked on his lover's dick until his cheeks hollowed out. Inside he felt a growing hunger as his demigod sucked on his balls while splaying his fingers on the back of Derek's thighs. Listening to the slurping sound coming from Titus between his legs sent him to the edge of sanity. He was mad with passion for this sexy immortal.

"Enough," Titus panted. "I want to be inside you, love."

He smiled and gazed into the multicolored orbs that had amazed him that first time he'd visited Love Ink. "I want that, too. More than I've ever wanted anything in all my life."

"You're a devil, aren't you?" Titus leaned to the left, reaching for the drawer of the nightstand by the bed. He brought out a bottle of lubricant. "I bet you're holding back those three precious words I so want to hear from you just to torture me. No matter. You will say them. Wait and see."

All his life he'd never let anyone in this close, not even his ex. Somehow Titus had opened him up wide until his very soul was exposed, and for the first time he wasn't afraid. Gazing into his immortal's eyes felt like home. Trust wasn't easy for him, but without it he would not know the full pleasure of being with Titus. *Say it, Derek. Don't be a chicken shit.*

Before he could speak, his lover flipped him onto his stomach. "Have you bottomed before, sweetheart."

"A long time ago."

"I thought so. I'll take my time. If you need me to slow down or even stop, just say so, okay?"

"Of course," he answered as Titus applied a generous amount of a slick substance to his backside.

"Your ass is something else, Detective. I can't wait to get inside your body."

His every cell burned as Titus sent a finger past the tight ring. When his immortal's lips landed on his ass cheeks, he ground his cock into the mattress trying to find relief, but none would come until his lover's cock was deep inside him. Anticipation rolled through him like a lusty hurricane.

Titus added another finger to the first intruder of his ass. The immortal's digits went in deeper, sliding against the spot that inflamed him even more. Mad for the final release, he fisted the sheets. "Take me now. Please."

"My pleasure, sweetheart." Titus positioned his cock between the cheeks of Derek's ass. "Ready?"

"Do it," he begged.

With a quick thrust, his lover's cock pierced past his ring, entering his body, joining them together as one. The pain was intense but faded away quickly. His lover's dick was massive, filling him utterly.

"You okay, sweetheart?" Titus asked, becoming still as a statue but keeping his cock seated deep inside his body.

"Yes. Fuck. You feel so good." He wanted to surrender everything to his sweet immortal. "Fuck me, Titus."

With slow, torturous strokes, his lover made him suffer deliciously.

"Baby, you feel incredible," Titus breathed. "Squeeze my dick. That's it. Wow. Perfect."

His immortal's thrusts came faster and rougher. Each stroke consumed more of him. In and out. Again and again. Titus's cock went in deeper and deeper still.

Derek rubbed the mattress with his hard cock as his lover brought him closer to climax. When he felt Titus reach around his waist and tighten his hand on his cock, he gasped. His immortal increased his dick's powerful thrusts back there and matched his hand's squeezing strokes on Derek's cock.

"You're close, aren't you, my love?" Titus asked in a lusty, hushed tone.

Before he could answer him, his balls unloaded, sending his hot liquid to his cock. Instantly, he shot his lusty load onto the silky sheets.

"Y-Yes," his lover growled, and with a final thrust he sent his cock even deeper into Derek's ass. He could feel the jerk of Titus's dick in his body as his darling beast sent hot jets of his seed into him.

Titus on top of him made him feel safe, cared for, and protected. This was the real heaven for him.

Titus pulled out of him and rolled to the side, pulling him into a spoon embrace. "I love you so much, my love."

His immortal's words were honest and heartfelt. This was where he belonged, in Titus's arms. This was his future, his forever.

Derek took a deep breath, closed his eyes, and for the first time in his life he said it. "I love you."

Titus's eyes widened and his flecks of silver and gold on his irises sparkled. "I thought I knew all there was to know about love, but I didn't know a damn thing. Not until you came into my shop. You, Derek taught me what true love is. For two hundred twenty-nine years I thought I was living, but I was wrong. Hearing you say those words, those three amazing eternal words just now, is like being born, breathing and seeing for the first time. Gods, I love you. I want you, now and forever by my side."

Derek smiled. "I've said it before and I'll say it again—you've got quite the lines, mister. I can't give you forever. I will grow old and you won't. What about that? What then? And don't try to change the subject, Mr. Love. It's a valid concern."

His immortal cupped his chin. "I will never leave you, my love. Ever. No matter what comes, I will remain by your side if you'll have me as your partner, your lover."

"Of course I'll have you. I was dead inside before you came into my life. You've given me so much. I see the world, no longer in black and white, but in every color of the rainbow. Yes, I'll be yours and you will be mine. I love you, my dear immortal."

"Isn't this a picture of sweetness," said a villainous voice that he didn't recognize. He felt Titus's body stiffen next to him.

He opened his eyes and saw the silvery net that now covered both of them. It stung his flesh, and numbed his body, paralyzing him. From the painful groans coming from Titus, he knew the evil thing caused his lover much more pain. He needed to act quickly. Was this the assassin sent to kill him? His gun was still under the pillow. Somehow he had to get his hand to move despite the goddamn net's obvious power to immobilize. Would his pistol even have any impact on an immortal? Probably not, but what other options were left him?

Looking directly at the intruder holding a gun in one hand and a twelve-inch blade in the other, he immediately recognized him. He'd seen the man with Barnes at some of the gay clubs over the past couple of months. Could this be Barnes's assistant? What was his name? *Think.* He'd read it in the file.

"Wiles Underwood?" he asked, hoping to gain an advantage.

"Who the fuck are you?" the insane creep asked.

Silently, Titus's voice whispered in the back of his mind. "Please let him hear me. Derek, be careful. This man is mortal but he's juiced up with divine fire. I've seen this kind of fire back in Spain a long time ago. He's either Promethean or he's working for them."

"I will. I can't move. Can you?" he sent, unsure if Titus could hear his mind. Aloud, he answered Wiles. "I'm just a friend. A mortal just like you."

A clear message from Titus came through. "Thank Olympus, the ambrosia has enhanced your oracle powers. That's why we can hear each other's thoughts. Listen, I'm completely frozen in place from this fucking Promethean net. I can't even speak aloud, Derek."

Wiles's eyes danced wildly in his head. "Did Ms. Carver send you, too? Since you can talk, you're not lying about being human. That uppity skank told me that this net thingy works on human beings, but it kicks some serious ass with these magical sons of bitches."

Derek could see the signs of drug use all over this bastard—greasy skin, needle tracks at the bends of his arms, but the biggest clue was the manic fidgeting. Wiles clearly had taken several hits from a pipe before coming here. His partner, Michael Vende, was the expert on how to deal with cracked out druggies. God, how he wished the OCD detective was here to help him figure a way out of this hornet's nest.

"You're here to get in on the power trade, too?" Wiles asked.

"Of course, Carver sent me. I'm here for the magic, just like you," he lied. "Mind taking this net off of me, buddy?"

The fucker placed the barrel of the gun to his forehead. "Yes. I mind very much, asshole. I'm not your buddy. I'm the one with the gun. I'm the one in charge here."

"No problem. We can wait for Carver to come and vouch for me."

"What makes you think the cunt is coming?"

"I don't know. I just figured you'd need her to get out of here." Derek wanted to keep him talking. Some clue on how to slip free of this trap might present itself. "Isn't she the one who helped you get here in the first place?"

"She did, but she also loaded me with enough of the good stuff to get back on my own." The psycho smiled wickedly, gazing at Titus. "I can't wait to deliver this super-duper energy booster and get my cut."

Derek's gut tightened. Whatever it took, he would keep Titus from being taken. "That's impressive, Wiles. Very impressive."

Titus's voice came to his mind. "Don't try to save me, love. This isn't your fight."

"You got a name?" Wiles asked, stepping back, scratching his ugly forehead with the barrel of his gun.

"Most call me Derek," he said aloud, while sending a silent thought to Titus. "The hell it's not. I love you. There's no way I'm letting this punk take you away from me."

"Why didn't Ms. Carver tell me about you?"

"Who knows with her? You said it. She's a skank." The longer he kept Wiles here, the better.

"I guess so. Haven't known her that long. Enjoyed the chat, bud, but I've got to get this superdude back to the bitch's hole. Nice to meet you, Derek. Hope you can figure a way out of here before you freeze to death." The maniac's thin lips twisted up into a gruesome smirk.

Panic took a front seat in Derek's mind. *Gotta stop this. Gotta get my pistol and stop this.* "Wiles, you better think twice about leaving. I wouldn't want you to piss off Ms. Carver on your first job."

"What are you talking about?"

He needed to get Wiles's mind off Titus. "I was sent to get the ambrosia on the table in the other room. There are several bottles. We only need to bring Carver a couple and you and I can split the rest."

"Ambrosia?"

"You're really new, aren't you? It's liquid magic. Fuck. It'll get you so fucking high, better than any ice you've ever smoked. That's for sure."

Wiles's eyes widened. He'd found the creep's weakness, and that might've bought them some more time. "How did you get hooked up with the Prometheans in the first place?"

"I don't know what you're talking about, dude. That fucking whore Carver is the one who turned me on to this job. My payoff for capturing pretty boy here is a whole bunch of his sweet energy, enough to last me the rest of my life, unlike those puny tats of his."

Wiles is the killer. Keep the fucker talking and we might stay alive. "I hear you. What a rush that's going to be." He silently questioned Titus. "Any suggestions?"

His lover's thought came through. "I'm trying to get a message out to Kyros and my other cousins, but I can't get it past this fucking net."

Derek sent the soundless message. "Keep trying, and I'll keep engaging this creep."

"Hooking up with Mr. Love must've been a trip," Wiles said.

"Major. I'm still buzzing from the stuff I got from him."

"You siphoned some power just by fucking him?"

No way was he letting Wiles come near Titus. Time to change the subject and fast. "God, I could really use a taste of that ambrosia." Running out of options, he mentally reached out to his mother's gift inside him. "Seriously, dude, you've got to take a hit from it. It'll knock your dick in the dirt."

"That fucking good, huh?"

To Derek's surprise, he was able to move his fingers slightly.

How? Likely his mother's power magnified by the ambrosia he'd consumed or by his sheer act of will. Whatever the reason, hope sprung to the forefront of his mind. "You bet it's off the fucking charts, Wiles. For real. How did you meet Carver? You must've done some pretty amazing shit to get on her good side." *If this bastard will just look away, I can get my gun. If he's really mortal, a bullet could fix this mess.*

"You have no idea."

"Someone like Carver is only impressed by the best. What did you do?" The smirk on the fucker's face sickened him, but he met it with a false smile. "Tell me, dude."

"No time. Sorry. Since you definitely won't be leaving with me and Mr. Love, I guess whatever treasures I find here are mine, not yours. Don't go anywhere." Wiles laughed and then turned to the door to the hallway, clearly to head to the kitchen to swipe the bottles of ambrosia.

This is my only chance to save Titus, heaven help me. He closed his eyes and opened himself fully to his mother's gift. His fingertips burned, and he reached for the gun. Miraculously, his arm moved. The bed creaked. *Damn.*

"Fucking asshole," Wiles yelled, twisting back around and aiming his weapon at Derek's chest.

In a single fluid motion, he pulled his Beretta out of the holster under his pillow, pointed it at Wiles, and squeezed the trigger. Time didn't slow down as it did in the movies, but Derek was aware that the killer he'd been searching for had just unloaded a couple of slugs into him. The impact from each bullet felt like someone had swung a sledgehammer into the middle of his chest.

Wiles's mouth was gapped open, his lips slack, his eyes empty. Relief washed over Derek when he saw the four holes his dear Beretta had created in the fucker—one in the center of his gut, two in his chest, and one just above Wiles's left eye. Titus was safe. The Prometheans would go without tonight.

In a daze, Derek brought his hand up to his face and saw dark red blood coating his fingertips. His vision clouded and his eyelids fell.

Titus's silent, single-syllable scream shook his core like a tornado. "No!"

Derek couldn't seem to open his eyes. "I love you, Titus. You're going to be okay." A thousand other things he wanted to tell his sweet immortal swirled in his head, but the blackness silenced him before he could.

~

TITUS SCREAMED AGAIN AND AGAIN, the Promethean net preventing any sound from leaving his mouth.

He'd never shed a single tear in his very long existence, but now they streamed down his face like rivers.

Derek, the love of his life, was dead.

The Promethean puppet bastard had killed him. Bitter justice was the psycho fucker was nothing more than a corpse on the floor filled with Titus's sweet detective's bullets.

How had Derek been able to move under the net? Willpower and his oracle bloodline had to be the reason. His entire being was crushed, flattened, thrashed to dust. Without Derek, he didn't want to live a single moment more. Once he got free of this goddamn net he would find the Prometheans, and one in particular, Ms. Carver, whoever she was. He would kill as many as he could until they overcame him and took his life.

A flash of red filled the room. Cole materialized next to the bed with his sword drawn. "What the fuck happened here?"

He sent a thought to Cole, hoping with him being so close he could receive it like Derek had been able to. "Don't touch the net. It's filled with Promethean magic." The whole world had changed for him now that Derek was gone. From now on, every breath would be a burden, every tick of a clock, hell.

"No shit." Cole shook his head. "This guy on the floor is Promethean?"

He pushed another message to his cousin. "Yes."

"And this is your detective, Titus." Cole used his sword to lift the net off of him.

Slowly, the paralyzing effect of the net faded. His mouth was the first to come back. "You came here to kill Derek, didn't you? How did you find us? This place is supposed to be a secret."

"It's not as secret as Notos seems to think. I had orders to kill Derek. I was just doing what I was told," Cole said. "You know we have to keep the family safe. I am sorry for your loss, cousin."

Gone? He's gone. My Derek is gone. He swallowed hard, choking back his tears, his rage, the best he could. "No. I don't accept that, Cole."

"Cousin, are you okay?"

"Fuck no, I'm not okay. The only man I've ever truly loved saved my life by sacrificing his own." As the last of the net's spell faded and his body was his again, he knelt beside Derek on the bed. "I don't accept any of this. It's not fair. None of it. He deserved better than this, better than me."

Grief-stricken, he stretched out on Derek's body.

"Titus, there's nothing you can do now. I'm sorry."

He turned and glared at Cole. "I don't accept that, cousin." Then drawing all the power inside him down his arms and into his fingers, he touched Derek's cheek. "Live, my love. Take all of me and live."

"No, Titus. You can't. It's impossible. If you drain yourself of everything, you will not survive."

"I must try. A single moment in a world without this man would burn me more than the hottest hellfire. I cannot bear living without him, Cole. If I can't save Derek, I will at least die trying to." Forcing more of his power out of his body and into his sweet detective, Titus felt his life draining out of him. Death was near. The energy left inside him couldn't fill a thimble. "Good-bye, Cole. Tell the family I'm so sorry."

"Wait, Titus."

"Don't try to stop me. I swear, I'll pound you into the ground cousin if you dare defy me." *Derek, I'm sorry about everything.* Titus willed the last remaining flicker of his power to his fingertips.

Just before he sent it into his lover's body, Cole grabbed his shoulder. "You've done it. I can't believe it. Your mortal lives. How do you feel?"

He didn't answer him, but looked down and saw his lover's eyes open. A miracle had ended his hellish nightmare. "My love, I'm here."

Derek's smile filled him with utter joy. "I love you, too, my sweet immortal."

12

Knowing his and Titus's lives were at stake once again had Derek on edge.

The large empty conference room they stood in, with the oversized mahogany table, plush leather chair, and digital clock on the wall didn't give him any comfort about what they were about to face.

He grabbed Titus's hand. "What's the protocol here?"

Waiting to meet his lover's family would've been tough enough in any case, but that they were the actual twelve Olympian Greek ruling gods and goddesses tossed his former worldview into the proverbial trash. That he and Titus were here to face the judgment and possible punishment of these immortals shoved him to the very brink of crazyville.

"I'm here, Derek. I'll take the lead and keep you on track. You sit there and only answer questions if asked. Don't offer up anything on your own." Titus touched his cheek, easing his concern a bit. "I promise I won't let them harm you."

"Really? You might've brought me back from the dead, sweetheart, but besting Zeus isn't in the cards and you know it." *Zeus. I'm actually about to meet him. Shit.*

"I'm not going to best him, love. If things look to be going against us, I'm going to teleport you out of here."

"Where is 'here' exactly?" He'd wondered ever since Titus had teleported them to this place.

"This isn't Olympus, if that's what you're asking. We're just outside London. This is one of many places my family meets for these kinds of things."

"How are you going to zap me out of here under the very noses of the gods?"

"With the help of my cousins, Uncle Notos, and my grandparents, sweetheart."

"How can they help you do that, Titus, since they are so far away?"

"There here," he whispered. "Just down the hall in the waiting room, love. That's not too far for them to transfer power to me. Kyros and Cole have set up a safe place for you where even the council won't find you. You'll be fine. I promise."

"Sounds like you're talking about a kind of divine witness protection program."

Titus shrugged. "Kind of."

"And what about you?" he asked his immortal lover.

"I'll face my family. I'm the one who broke our laws, not you."

Before he could argue that Titus wasn't the only one in trouble here and that he, though only a mere human, wasn't about to let him face the firing squad alone, in walked a very attractive woman.

Most would've thought the beauty to be in her late twenties, but he'd learned the people in Titus's family didn't exhibit their incredible ages. She wore jeans, a black top, and black stilettos. The woman's blonde hair was long, quite long. Though he wasn't lusting after her curves, he had to admire their symmetry and form. Her stunning looks would've fit perfectly on the most sought-after catwalks of the world, causing even overly confident supermodels to fall to the ground into fetal positions.

His psychic powers warmed at the very sight of her, and he could sense the strong connection between her and Titus. Something about her presence also gave Derek hope that things tonight might, after all they'd been through, actually turn out okay for him and Titus.

"Hello, gentlemen." Her voice sounded lyrical and warm and reached into him with several clear notes of promise.

"My lady," Titus said, bending at the waist and lowering his eyes to the floor.

Derek followed suit, but with his eyes unmoving from her and with his mouth remaining silent.

She broke the silence first. "Titus, let's put formality aside."

His lover stood up straight. "I'm not sure all will agree with you on a casual approach for this hearing."

"They will." She nodded. "I'm very persuasive when I need to be, and apparently I really need to be in this situation. Besides, Hera and I already spoke. She sides with me on keeping things informal. Introduce me to your mortal." Her gaze turned away from his companion to him. Her eyes were like Titus's, multicolored with flecks of silver and gold. "Pardon me. Of course I mean your friend, Titus."

"This is Detective Derek Stone, my lover." Titus squeezed his hand and he squeezed back. "This is my great-grandmother, Eros's mother, Aphrodite, goddess of Love."

His jaw dropped and then snapped shut. No amount of preparing could've helped with this event. How old could Aphrodite be? At the very least, four thousand years, maybe more. He sure wasn't about to ask her. Asking someone's age was rude likely even here. How powerful? He certainly didn't want to find out.

"Detective Stone, a pleasure to meet you," she said and sat down in one of the seats. "I'm feeling fairly confident that this will go your way." Her sudden smile softened his worry some. "I've got my fingers crossed for you."

She sounded sincere, though he couldn't know for sure. Immortals had the advantage of time to hone their skills of subterfuge and deception. "Thank you, ma'am. I'm pleased to meet you, too."

"Please call me, Aphrodite, Detective Stone."

"And you call me, Derek, please." He couldn't help but like the goddess. She was charming.

"I will do that for sure." She looked back at Titus. "Did you get my message that I sent through Hermes's son-in-law?"

"You mean Uncle Notos?"

She nodded.

"Yes. I know the family is more than a little pissed off about everything, especially about the murders that linked to Love Ink."

"That's true, but did he tell you that you've got some supporters on the Dodekatheon?" she asked.

Derek turned to Titus. "Dodekatheon? What's that?"

"It's the name of the ruling body of my family." His lover shook his head. "No, I didn't hear that message. Do we have enough support?" Titus asked her.

"I'm not sure. It'll be a very close vote. You know the law. Exposure to humanity is a big no-no with us elders, if not the biggest."

Titus nodded. He knew.

"Make yourself comfortable, Derek," Aphrodite said. "The others should be here shortly. You too, Titus."

As he and Titus sat down, three gods wearing stylish corporate suits and power ties walked in. Titus whispered their names to him. Like Aphrodite's entrance had impacted him positively, so did Apollo's, Dionysus's, and Hermes's. Bliss and wonder were the emotions evoked inside him by their very presence.

Quite attractive, youthful-looking males, the three ancient gods took their seats around the table.

Apollo, an extremely handsome black man, didn't even acknowledge them, but began looking at what Derek assumed was a text, email, or game on his cell. Even with his gift, Derek couldn't tell what the god of light was thinking. Apollo's vote could definitely go either way.

His blond-haired companions, Dionysus and Hermes, sat together and chatted quietly about some stock pick they'd both made recently. The glares they sent him told him definitely where they were going to cast their votes, and they weren't going to be in his and Titus's favor.

"Here comes Demeter," his lover whispered.

In a simple white dress, the red-headed goddess of harvest stepped into the room, her green eyes practically shooting daggers.

"Titus, by the looks of these members of your family, I count one positive vote in our column, three against, and one undecided."

"I agree, but there are seven more on the counsel. Let's wait and see before we throw in the towel, love. We only need seven to win. Here come more elders."

Derek looked up and saw four more members of the ruling body of gods entering the room.

Titus leaned his way. "The guy leading the pack in the Valentino suit with the dark hair and matching beard is Poseidon."

The wink from the god of the seas alleviated some of his apprehension. Likely, Poseidon would side with them once the vote was taken.

"The woman behind him in the camo is Athena," Titus continued. "She and Ares are at odds about something that happened in 1909."

"What?" he asked quietly, while noticing the goddess frown. Mentally, he noted the current possible vote to come. *Two up. Four down. One on the fence.* Fuck, things needed to turn around fast or they'd be on the losing side of this conclave.

"No one knows but Athena and Ares. They had seats next to each other on the counsel for thousands of years, but now they refuse to be that close to one another. The woman smiling at us is Artemis, Apollo's twin sister."

The woman looked ravishing with marvelous curves, raven hair, and ebony skin.

Her smile helped their tally. *Three for, four against, and one unknown.*

The next of the gods to arrive had a cane, which he found odd. "Who is that?"

"Hephaestus, god of fire. He's married to Aphrodite," Titus informed as the man took a seat next to his beautiful wife. The lame deity grinned at them, ticking off another box. *Four to four with Apollo's vote still clouded.*

"Hephaestus is your great-grandfather then?"

His lover shook his head. "No. He is." Titus pointed to the man invading the space dressed in all black with holstered pistols at both his sides. "Ares is my great-grandfather."

"I should've remembered that from my earlier investigation and research into Barnes's and Crane's murders. Your grandfather's parents are Aphrodite and Ares."

"That's right."

"I'm surprised Hephaestus seems to be leaning to our side."

Titus put his arm around his shoulders. "Love, my family's past is something they've had to learn to deal with. There are way too many skeletons in their closets for them not to have."

Ares sat down between Demeter and Apollo. Like the later, Derek didn't have a sense where the god's vote would land.

"Hello," the regal woman walking into the space said. "How is everyone?" She wore a black suit, perfectly tailored for her body.

"We're fine, Hera. How are you?" Demeter asked the gorgeous female.

"Our queen," Titus whispered.

"I'm excellent, sister," Hera answered Demeter.

"What do you think of my great-grandson, my queen?" Aphrodite asked.

The goddess sighed. "I'm going to wait for my ex to show before I make known my will on this matter."

"Ex?" he whispered to Titus.

"Yes. She and Zeus divorced a long time ago."

"That's not in anything I've read."

"There's a lot in your mythic records about my family that isn't there or is flat wrong."

"I can't wait to learn more about them," Derek said, wishing to give his lover some hope about how this was going to turn out.

All eleven of the Olympian deities busted the ten-scale on looks, hitting twelves and thirteens. Even with their divine beauty, Derek thought the whole scene looked more like the boardroom of a global conglomerate than the counsel of gods and goddesses.

Still, one chair remained empty at the head of the table. It didn't take his psychic gift to tell him that seat was for Zeus, the king of the gods.

All the Olympians looked to the door expectantly. He did the same, feeling hope drain from him as he checked the current count. Four of the immortals seemed to be leaning their direction, and four more the other way. Apollo, Ares, and Hera were playing their cards close to the vest.

When their king didn't show immediately, the gods and goddesses began filling their glasses with water from the crystal pitchers that had been placed on the table for them. Titus grabbed the one closest to them and poured drinks for both of them.

Derek's throat felt like the desert, so he took his glass and downed half its contents in a single gulp. When he sat it back down on the table, he felt a cold chill slide down his backbone.

"Hades, what a pleasant surprise to see you here," Hera said. "We weren't expecting you."

He glanced up at the god of the underworld. The image Hades presented was incongruent with what his mother's gift was telling him. The god wore jeans and a long-sleeved, light blue shirt. His blond hair was wavy. His feet—or hooves, perhaps—were inside tennis shoes. Only Hades' dark eyes aligned with the frantic wave of red in the back of his mind.

"You wouldn't have, sister. I only informed Zeus a few moments ago of my intentions to be here."

"Shall I conjure a chair for you, brother?" the god of the seas asked.

"Thank you, but I prefer to stand." The death god moved to the far corner, leaned against the wall, and fixed his black eyes on Derek.

He thought about looking away, but the shiver that went through his body made him unable to turn his gaze away. "Titus, does he have a vote?"

"Not exactly."

Before he could ask him to clarify, Demeter spoke. "All stand for our king."

"You can't be serious," Hera said, the only one of those in the room remaining seated.

Already standing on his feet, Derek glanced at Zeus, who unlike the other immortals looked his age, which was clearly extremely ancient. The divine sovereign's locks were snow white, as was his beard. The noble took the seat directly across from Titus and him. Dread consumed Derek completely.

"You've got to be kidding me." The king's ex rolled her eyes. "Father Christmas called, and he would like his image back."

"Don't start with me, Hera," Zeus snapped.

The heavenly ruler's form changed into that of a much younger beardless man.

Derek leaned to his lover's ear. "You're not telling me that Santa Claus is real, too, are you?"

Titus shrugged, and then nodded.

"Order. Come to order," Zeus pounded his fist on the wooden table. A hush came over the room. "We are here to decide on the guilt or innocence of one of our own. Is the accused present?"

"May the ancients save me," Hera said. "Of course he's here, Zeus. I propose we forgo the old conventions. Who agrees with me?"

"I do," Aphrodite said.

"Damn it, Hera. You're not running this counsel," the king of the gods said. "I am."

"Brother, I'm with her." Poseidon leaned forward. "If we follow norm we'll be here forever. Allow a vote to put aside the ancient practices. It will speed up this process. You and I can be at the driving range in under an hour. What do you say?"

"Fine. With a show of hands, who agrees with our queen?"

All but Demeter and Zeus raised their hands.

"Titus, do you know why you're here?" Zeus asked.

Derek watched his brave lover stand.

"Yes, my king. I broke several of our laws. I stole my grandfather's arrow and made magical ink. With the ink I helped some mortals in need."

"Yes, my son. You did." Zeus nodded. "And three mortals are dead at the hands of a Promethean."

"That's not entirely accurate," Ares said. "The killer acted alone at first. The Prometheans reached out to him after the fact."

Derek thought the count might be tipping their direction. Ares seemed to be siding with them, no longer in the undecided column.

"But the Prometheans did use him," Zeus said. "This Wiles fellow didn't have any means to go to Notos's Antarctica retreat otherwise."

Demeter nodded. "I understand Ares sent Cole to find and dispose of this mortal sitting next to Titus."

"His name is Derek Stone, my lady." Titus glared at the goddess.

"Yes. I know who he is and how dangerous it is for him to still be alive. Anyway, Cole had trouble locating him. How did our enemies find him and Titus so easily?"

"I can answer that," Aphrodite said. "Notos and my son, Eros, went over everything in the cabin with a fine-tooth comb. When they found that Detective Stone's badge had been enchanted with a beacon spell, they went to his workplace to continue their investigation. It turns out that Derek's commander is a card-carrying Promethean."

Derek was shocked to hear that. "Lieutenant Gray? That's not possible."

"It's not only possible, it's the truth, Derek," the goddess said. "According to some notes our team found, Gray had been watching you ever since he realized you were an oracle. He was long gone when our people showed up. He'll turn up somewhere eventually, and when he does, we'll be there. I'm sure he would've eventually tried to convert you over to his side. Oracles are highly sought after in the Order's circles. This Wiles Underwood fellow's ancestors were from Delphi itself. Descendants have unique gifts Prometheans need to continue their evil deeds."

"I wouldn't have ever joined those bastards."

"I believe you, Derek. Because of you we have our first intel in many years about our enemies. We have two names now—your former commander's and a Ms. Daphne Carver. Thank you for that."

"I still can't believe Gray is working with the Prometheans."

"You might be surprised, Detective, to learn just how many of the people in seats of power in your world are aligned with those bastards," Ares said.

Aphrodite continued. "Eventually, your commander would have killed you, Derek, had you refused his offer to join the ranks of the Prometheans. There's no doubt about that. Your life would've been over had you not met my great-grandson."

"I didn't have a life before him." He reached for his immortal's hand. Titus squeezed his fingers tenderly.

"Enough," Zeus hit the table with his open palm. "Quiet. Everyone." The king of the gods stared straight at him, causing a shiver to shoot down his spine. "Detective Stone, you need to understand something. Mortals are not allowed to speak here."

Zeus's anger didn't bode well for him and Titus.

"Brother, permission to speak." Hades stepped forward.

"Of course."

"Detective Stone has every right to be heard here," the god of the dead said.

Hera sighed. "Why do the males in this family love to hear themselves speak? Get to the point, please."

Hades smiled, causing Derek's blood to chill. "Derek William Stone died yesterday."

"What game are you playing, brother?" Zeus asked.

"Ares, if you don't mind," the ruler of the underworld said.

The god of war nodded and waved his hand. Cole materialized, standing just behind Ares.

"Thank you," Hades said to Ares. The death god looked directly at Cole. "Tell your family what you told me and your grandfather, young man."

The demigod, Titus's cousin, sent to kill him recounted what Derek already knew had happened at the cabin. Somehow, Titus was able to bring him back from the dead. The gunshot wounds Wiles had given him were gone, and not a single scar remained.

"Impossible," Apollo said.

"No way," Hermes chimed in.

Several of the others seemed to agree.

Zeus shook his head. "This mortal must've only appeared dead. That kind of power hasn't been in play since we retreated from humankind. Titus was consuming a little extra ambrosia. That's all. He has no temple, no followers. To raise someone up from the dead would take a couple of thousand mortals' adoration at least."

"Maybe so, brother. But it did happen." Hades's unwavering stare on Derek felt like it reached into his very soul. "In truth, these two actually saved each other. Detective Stone shot and killed the Promethean agent who would've abducted this young immortal otherwise." The god of death raised his hand up and the ghost of Wiles Underwood appeared. The killer's spirit cowered back from Hades. "Did you kill this man, Mr. Underwood?"

The wispy image of Wiles glared at Derek and nodded.

"Thank you. Be gone." Hades waved his hand and the creep vanished. "The dead cannot lie to me, brother. You know that to be true."

"I still don't see your point," Zeus said. "Even if Titus was able to do the impossible and pull his lover's spirit back from your realm, what does that change about this proceeding? He's a mortal with unique knowledge of our existence. That makes him a danger to our family. The law is clear. He must be executed."

"No," Titus stood and yelled. "Never." He raised his hands up, clearly about to invoke a spell.

"How dare you threaten us." Zeus got up on his feet, and the room filled with sparks.

"Relax, brother. Eros's grandson is following his heart. Remember how it was to be young?" Hades turned to Titus. "And you, demigod of love, don't be a fool. Trust me. Your lover will not be terminated."

"For the love of Olympus, get to the point," Hera said.

The death god nodded. "Of course, my dear. There's one thing I know that no one else here knows."

"And that is?" Zeus asked.

"I'm not sure how Titus's transference of power was able to save his lover. Maybe since Detective Stone is descended from the oracles and has his own gift inside him the magic worked exponentially, better than anyone could ever imagine."

"I'm not buying this," Apollo snapped.

"That's perfect since I'm not selling anything, just putting forth some possibilities of how this phenomenon, this miracle, might have transpired."

"Your point is made, brother. Still, it has no bearing on this case. Titus broke our laws. This human is a risk to all immortals." Zeus's manner was quite similar to that of a lead politician. Working with these gods and goddesses must've been a lot like herding cats. "So, if you will please let us continue, I would be forever in your debt."

"One last item, for this esteemed counsel to consider." Hades turned and addressed him directly. "Derek, the miracle only began with your resurrection. The end result of this marvel you and Titus somehow accomplished together is what is most surprising, even to me. You're now one of us."

"I'm sorry, but I don't understand."

"My family can't do anything to you now. Your mortality has been stripped away and you are now immortal just like them. Just like all of us."

DEREK SAT on the couch of Love Ink next to his immortal lover, Titus, demigod of love. Around the room were his cousins and co-conspirators.

"I can't believe the elders confiscated all our ambrosia stash," Atreus said. "What good is having them bless our venture if we don't have the juice to accomplish anything?"

Krystal frowned. "They didn't exactly give us their seal of approval. We're under probation."

"I wish I could've been there to hear them fight about what we've done," Zil said.

"A split vote for now," Daemon said, sending a chill down Derek's spine. The guy reminded him too much of his grandfather, the god of death. "We screw things up and we could lose the support we got yesterday."

"Like I told you all before, this is a probationary trial," Titus said. "Aphrodite and Hera were our champions. We owe them for arguing our case."

"I love my grandmother." Jayson smiled. "She understands better than most that going against one's nature is wrong. We're Olympians. We're meant to aid mortals."

"And how do we do that if we don't have enough ambrosia to power up beyond the normal stuff?" Lukus asked.

"We need to figure out how our cousin pulled Derek back from death, that's how," Cole stated.

Kyros looked directly at him and Titus. "I still don't know how you did what you did. Detective, you should be dead."

Without a care that his cousins were present, Titus brazenly kissed him. Then he turned to Kyros. "I think love, our love for each other, had a lot to do with saving my sweet detective. More so than anyone knows, not even our elders."

Derek's cell buzzed. He read the message from Vende. *Deputy Chief Moore is looking for you.* "I've got to get back to the unit, guys."

"I can't believe you're going to keep your old job now that you know what you know and are what you are," Zil said.

"Believe it. Besides, I think having more eyes and ears on the police force is a good thing."

"And you were able to fix everything with Barnes's and Crane's deaths so that Titus didn't get arrested. It is great to have someone on the inside," said Kyros.

Derek rose from the couch. "Yes. It helped that Hades let us have Wiles's body. Still, the department bought the story I told them, and that's all that matters."

"Absolutely." Krystal smiled. "You're certainly not dead. How does it feel to be immortal, Detective?"

He turned to Titus and touched his cheek. This man was his future, his life. He'd never really lived until him. Now that forever was theirs to discover together, the possibilities seemed limitless. "Honestly, it's pretty sweet, Krystal." He kissed Titus and then whispered, "I love you."

"I love you, too, Derek." His immortal stood and embraced him. "I'll see you later at home."

~

Underground Compound, Canadian Rockies, Present

Gray walked by his mistress, praying silently for mercy.

"Where is this detective?" the high priestess asked quietly, though he was certain a storm of rage brewed underneath her false calm. His failure to bring the oracle into the fold would be a black mark on his record.

"He's still working from what our sources tell me, my lady. He and the demigod are an item apparently."

They came to *the door.*

"What about the other seer, Wiles Underwood? Any sign of him?" Her tone was soft and sweet.

"None. I gave him the net and told him how to invoke the tracking spell I placed on Stone's badge just like you commanded me."

Lady Carver waved her hand in front of the door. The charge in the air was hot. His mistress reached for the handle and twisted it, pushing the door open. Gray knew that if anyone touched it without the right incantations, they would be incinerated on the spot. Only seven of the highest of the faithful were privy to those spells, and Daphne Carver was one of them.

"Shall I follow you, my lady?"

"Of course, my son." The high priestess walked into the dark chamber, and Gray followed closely behind. "As you know, you must be punished for your defeat. You lost two important people. The abilities the two men possessed would have been valuable to the Order."

Dread rolled through him. "Mistress, please forgive me."

"No need, child. You're already forgiven." Carver raised her hands and the illumination in the room grew brighter, reflecting beautifully on her blonde curls.

Gray's jaw dropped. The source of all the Order's most ancient and powerful magics was less than five feet from them. "Prometheus?"

"The one and only. Take a good look at him."

The god of knowledge was stretched out on a stone table in chains. His eyes, glassy, stared into space.

"Is he still alive?"

"Yes, he is. Barely. But that's why we're here."

"I don't understand." A thought shot through him, not his own but one from another. One word swirled in his head, filling him with fright.

"This fool is our living battery. We have others but they are nothing compared to him. Nymphs and satyrs only last a decade or two, if we're lucky, and the power we get from them is good for a few tricks and some illusions but nothing more."

"Yes, mistress. I know our creed. Forgive me, but what I don't understand is why you brought me here. Punishments are normally doled out in a great convocation, to keep the faithful in line. I bow to your judgment, gladly offering myself as an example for the Order." Again, the single word sliced his consciousness.

Daphne's tone sharpened, reminding him of a razor. "You believe a leather whip to your back is what you deserve?"

He lowered his eyes. "I beg for your mercy, my lady." Again, the word clanged like a bell in his mind.

"Mercy? Interesting thought. The mission you were on has changed everything for the Order. The gods are still here. We always suspected it but could never find any proof. Caution is the name of the game now. Much caution." Carver waved her right hand and a baseball bat materialized in it. "In time we won't need this bag of crap any longer." She hit the chained god in the shin with the bat. The immortal didn't make a sound, even though the strike must've broken his bones. It was well known that Prometheus's body healed every twenty-four hours, but how and why, no one other than those at Daphne's rank really knew. The other gods dined on ambrosia to sustain their immortal lives.

"So my mission produced some advantage for us, your grace?" Again, the word blasted through him.

"Yes, Gray. We will bring down the immortals, taking their places as gods in this world. For now, we must keep this worthless fucker alive a little longer. That, my son, is why you are here."

The word screamed in the back of his head like an exploding bomb, but he could no longer move. The high priestess had evidently placed a spell on Gray that paralyzed him completely.

She sighed. "I'm so disappointed we lost our net. That was a powerful weapon."

He wanted to beg for mercy, forgiveness, whatever it would take for Daphne not to punish him. But besides being unable to move, he couldn't speak either.

"This Olympian bastard hates living more than any creature that has ever existed. In the beginning, he longed for vengeance. Now, I'm sure he prays for death to come. My job is to make sure it never does. You know what Prometheus's real weakness is, Gray? Of course you don't. It's us. Humans. Mortals. Long ago he cared too much and this is the price he paid. We almost lost the immortal bastard after only a few hundred years. Our inventory of the divine food had run out when one of our lowly priests figured a way to keep him alive. Blood. That's all it takes. Human blood."

Gray watched the bat transform into a sharp metal sickle. Carver looked like the queen of death.

"Thank you for your service to our Order, my son. Your sacrifice will be remembered. You will be missed." As Daphne swung the blade to his neck, Gray wished he'd heeded the word that he now knew had come from the chained god. That word had been 'run.'

THE END

ABOUT THE AUTHOR

Lee Swift, who writes under several pen names including Kris Cook, creates novels, short stories, screenplays and more.

With an unquenchable thirst to experience all his life journey has to offer, Lee and hubby love travel but still call Dallas, Texas home.

Join [HERE] to get updates on Lee.

ALSO BY LEE SWIFT

Novels

Morvicti Blood *(Supernatural Thriller)*

Cupid's Arrow *(Gay Fantasy Romance)*

Three to Play *(Menage MMF Romance)*

(All series listed in best reading order)

Mockingbird Place

(Gay Romance Series)

The Marine in Unit A

The Cowboy in Unit E

The Fireman in Unit C

The Doctor in Unit H

The Fighter in Unit J

Holiday Beaus (Novella)

The Musician in Unit G

The Cop in Unit B

Wolf Pack

(Menage MFM Romance Trilogy)

Secret Cravings

Primal Desires

Delicious Hunger

Eternal Trio Series

(Gay Menage Fantasy Romance)

Levi's Rogues

Perfection

<u>Writing with Lana Lynn</u>

(Thrillers)

Lexi's Protector *(Men Without A Cause)*

Liz's Guardian *(Men Without A Cause)*

<u>**Secret Diary**</u> Series as Kris Cook

(Erotic Straight BDSM Trilogy)

Mia's Spanking Diary

Misty's Bondage Diary

Lea's Ménage Diary

www.ingramcontent.com/pod-product-compliance
Lightning Source LLC
Chambersburg PA
CBHW022027170626
46808CB00003B/1087